MURDER IN THE EVENING

BLYTHE BAKER

～

Death comes to dine...

When an elegant dinner party with friends ends in the sudden death of a beautiful young socialite, Alice Beckingham finds herself a witness to murder. Intrigued by a cryptic note in which the victim predicts her own demise, Alice enlists the aid of the cunning but slippery Sherborne Sharp to investigate.

Alice has more than one killer to contend with, however, as her family continues to be plagued by unanswered questions surrounding an older unsolved mystery.

Working together, the lady detective and her jewel thief partner set out to trap a killer. But will the looming shadows of the past leave Alice blind to the dangers of the present?

～

1

Sitting alone in the room that had belonged to my brother, I thought there was very little of Edward remaining in the space anymore. Most of his personal items had been packed away out of sight long ago and a thin layer of dust coated the furnishings, as though the servants did not come in to clean very often. I did not blame them. A feeling of gloom hung over the space.

Heavy drapes blocked out any light from the windows. An unpleasant chill seemed to hang in the air, no matter that there was no reason for this room to be colder than any other in the house. It was all so still. Only the muffled noise of traffic filtering up from the London streets below disrupted the illusion of total isolation.

That was why I had come here, to sit quietly on the edge of the bed and be alone with my thoughts. Memories floated close to the surface. I did not have to skim very deep to find the one I sought, a memory of the afternoon that had changed the lives of everyone in my family forever...

I could still see the police officers leaving the house, their faces long and serious. They lowered their heads as they stepped through the door and onto the front steps. My father stood in the doorway, watching them walk down the path for a few moments before closing the door, shutting us all inside with the misery.

Sorrow thickened the air like smoke, making it difficult to breathe.

That familiar feeling came back to me every time I thought about that day. As though it was happening all over again. As though no time had passed at all.

Edward had been killed.

The police delivered the news as gently as possible, but a blow to the head can hardly be delivered delicately. No matter the intention, it hits you like a train, knocking you back and stealing your breath.

I was young then, though more than old enough to know what was going on. Mama and Papa tried to shield me, sending me away to my room, but I sat on the stairs and listened as they cried and talked and cried.

I had never seen my father cry before. Not at funerals or the births of children. But I learned that day that my father would cry over the loss of his own child—a scenario too macabre for me to have ever dreamed up.

Nothing that was happening made any sense to me. How could Edward have committed the awful crime he had confessed to? And how could he have been killed so soon after? All that I felt at the time was confusion, grief, and dread.

As I was sitting in Edward's room now, the house was

filled with a similar sense of foreboding and my thoughts were overflowing with very similar questions.

It had been two years since Edward's death in prison and there were still so many unknown details. We did not know who had killed him or why. At the time, the prison staff told us it had been the outcome of a fight.

But why had they been fighting? Had Edward started it? Was he attacked by another inmate?

Prior to his crimes, I would have told anyone who asked that Edward was a gentle young man. He could be provoked to anger and fits of yelling on occasion, but normally they were deserved. And if not, the fits were rare. Even the murder he had committed had been, in a twisted way, intended to protect our sister Catherine from ruin. Edward had poisoned Catherine's disreputable suitor, resulting in a violent scene that had ended with Edward's imprisonment and trial for the crime of murder.

But I could not imagine that Edward had been harboring violent fantasies all along. In truth, he had a similar disposition to our father. They were both serious, rarely smiling, and withheld many facts about their own lives even from the women who loved them.

And so, it was far easier to believe my brother had simply snapped and exhibited behavior very out of his own character. That thinking lent itself, then, to a difficulty understanding how or why he would get into a prison fight.

The guards on duty had few answers for us, and since he was a known murderer, there was little outcry about his violent end. Edward had fallen out of good society and lost the concern of the upper classes. His death made headlines, but many of the stories I managed to read despite my parents' best efforts simply said that justice had been served, even if at the hands of another inmate.

It did not feel like justice for my family, though. It felt like we had lost Edward twice. Once when he killed Catherine's suitor at our country house in Somerset and again when he lost his own life. It was a devastating blow we nearly did not overcome.

But we did.

We rallied together and had done our best in the previous two years to stay cheerful about the prospect of a future without Edward. We could still laugh and smile. Such things were not an insult to his memory. We did not need to remain miserable forever because he had made mistakes and paid the ultimate price for them.

While we succeeded most often in going about our lives, it felt tremendously more difficult on his birthday.

Mama always had the cooks make a large two-tiered cake on our birthdays, candles sticking out of the top for every year we had been alive. Edward hated listening to us sing. More often than not, he would extinguish the candles before we could finish singing because he didn't like so much attention being placed on him.

And when he opened gifts, he would lower his face and try not to smile, as though it would be embarrassing for him to be at all pleased about what he received.

"This was unnecessary," he'd say when he was finished, waving his arms to the table full of discarded wrapping paper and half-eaten slices of cake. "Wholly unnecessary."

Mama would insist that he was worth every ounce of effort and Papa would slap him on the back, a rare expression of fondness between the two of them. It was always a warm day in the house where Edward smiled more than normal and everything felt light.

Since his death, darkness followed the anniversary of his birth.

Even the days leading up to it were grim.

The week before felt like walking towards a large precipice knowing you had no way to stop. No matter how much you wanted to, you would keep walking until suddenly, you were plunging for the craggy bottom without so much as an umbrella to slow your fall.

Then, the days after would be a slow climb out of the pit and back to the light. I knew the reprieve would come, but until then, I sat in Edward's room and did my best to remember him fondly.

Because most of his things had been boxed up and removed, the room was barer than it ever was when he lived here. While alive, he kept books and pens and folded up newspapers lying around the room at all times. Even when the maid came to tidy up, he would instruct her to leave his personal things alone, meaning she could do little more than make his bed and dust around the mess.

Now, the clutter had been cleaned and sheets had been thrown over the furniture to protect it from disuse. Catherine had found love again some time ago and, during her wedding, the room had been used for storage. A few boxes of decorations lingered near the closet.

The place hardly felt familiar any more, and I stood slowly to my feet, taking one last look around the room before I quietly left.

The upstairs hallway was quiet, and I could see a light

coming from under my mother's door at the end of the hall. Since our recent visit to Druiminn Castle, she had scarcely left the house. She swore it had nothing to do with the murder that occurred while we were there, but I knew better than to believe her. Comforting the parents of a deceased young man had weighed heavily on her heart and mind, reminding her too much of her own weeks and months spent mourning.

Since returning, she had made excuses to cancel social gatherings and remain inside. Papa didn't mind. He was glad to stay home and catch up on his reading. He had never been one to enjoy social gatherings anyway.

It frustrated me to no end that he could not see that his own wife was struggling, but there was nothing I could say to convince him there was a problem, so I had given up.

I walked to the end of the hall and knocked on Mama's door.

"Come in," she called.

The room was brightly lit and my mother was sitting at her writing desk, pen poised in the air.

"I didn't mean to interrupt you."

"Never," she said, smiling and replacing the pen in the cup at the corner of the desk. "I was just writing to Catherine. I know she told me when she would be coming for a visit soon, but I can't for the life of me remember what day she said."

She looked to me in hopes I remembered, but I shook my head. "I didn't even know she was coming for a visit."

Mama shrugged and turned to me. "You look lovely."

I grabbed the silk material of my dress and held it out, looking down to admire the blue gown. "I was invited to dinner tonight with a few friends. It has been a while since I've been out, so I wanted to look nice."

"I remember you going out just a few nights ago," she said, eyebrow raised. "Is that 'awhile' for the youth now?"

"You are the one who raised me to maintain a bustling social calendar," I said, hoping to gently broach the subject of my mother reemerging into society.

"Then I taught you well." She pushed away from the desk and walked over to me slowly, wincing at her right hip before it worked itself out and she could stand fully upright. "I fear I am getting old."

"You look the same to me." It was only a partial lie. Until recently, my mother had looked as young and beautiful as ever. The gray beginning to appear in her hair made her look rather distinguished, and despite the passage of time, she always seemed to glow with a youthful kind of radiance.

Recently, however, she had grown pale and tired looking, as though she was perpetually lacking sleep.

I knew part of it had to do with the arrival of Edward's birthday and part of it had to do with the recent death we'd experienced while away in Scotland. But it was still shocking to see such a sudden change in her appearance, as though her inward struggle couldn't help but manifest itself physically.

"I will walk you to the door," she said. "I need to speak with your father, anyway. Perhaps he knows when Catherine is coming to visit."

"Unlikely." We walked down the hallway and towards the stairs together, my hand patting her arm as though we were two old friends rather than mother and daughter.

She laughed softly. "You are right, but the moment I stop asking him is the moment I will lose all hope of him paying attention to anything I or anyone around him says. He won't feel even the smallest obligation to listen when someone speaks. He will just disappear behind his newspaper and forget the world."

Since Edward died and Catherine left, my mother and I had grown closer together. For much of my youth, we were at odds. I was always too silly or too loud or too unmannered.

All of those things were still true half of the time, but my mother's tolerance for them had seemed to grow now that I was her last child in the house. She still treated me like a child from time to time, which forced me to act like one in rebellion, but otherwise, our relationship had found a kind of ease that didn't exist when I was younger.

When we reached the first-floor landing, my mother pulled her arm from me and leaned her head into my father's study.

"James?"

When he didn't answer, she moved to the other side of the room, looking into the sitting room. "James?"

"No need to shout, dear. I'm right here." He walked out of the library, a book held open in his hands. "What is the emergency?"

"No emergency. Your daughter is leaving for the night."

He looked up and nodded to me. "Have fun."

"You don't care where she is going?" she asked.

He sighed. "I presume you asked her where she was going, and you would not be allowing her to leave if you thought it inappropriate."

My mother opened her mouth to respond, but I interrupted before she could. "I am going out with friends, and as an adult, I don't really require permission any longer."

At that, my father turned to me, eyes narrowed. "We know the friends you are meeting?"

"Violet Colburn and her group," I said. "Mama has met them before."

"Oh, of course," she said. "Lovely girls. It will be good for you to get out of the house."

The reason remained unspoken between the three of us. Although we were each aware of the date and what it meant, no one dared discuss it. I thought talking about Edward might relieve the gloom in the house, but it was obvious my parents disagreed. And if it was easier for them to get through today without addressing the reason behind their sadness, I did not want to make things worse for them.

"I should get going before I am late," I said.

"Take your coat," my mother said, grabbing it from a closet in the hall. "It is growing chillier, especially in the evenings."

I did not have time to argue, so I shrugged into the sleeves of the long coat and adjusted my cloche hat over my cropped brown curls. "It has been a time since I've seen Violet and the girls, so I may not be right home after dinner."

"Have fun," my mother said from the doorway, waving as I walked down the front path.

Our chauffeur, George, was waiting at the curb with the car, the door already opened for me.

"Thank you, George," I said, taking his hand and allowing him to help me into the backseat.

When we pulled away, my mother was still watching from a crack in the door, as though she wished she were coming with me.

Just before we reached the end of the block, I saw the crack of light escaping from the house disappear, and I knew she had gone back inside.

2

Dorothy Thompson arrived at the table with her coat hanging halfway off her shoulder and the back of her hand pressed to her forehead.

"I am so sorry I am late," she said, cheeks flushed as red as her hair. "Reginald came home from work late, and he didn't have a key to the house, so I could not leave until he came home because the house couldn't be locked up and—"

"It seems married life and your expectant condition are suiting you just fine," I said, pulling out her chair as she removed her coat and handed it to the man who had been at the front desk, but had since followed Dorothy all the way across the restaurant in an attempt to check her coat and bag. He took it from her with a forced smile, his eyes betraying his annoyance.

"Oh, yes," she beamed, scooting in and reaching for the glass of ice water on the table. "Everything is wonderful."

"Good. We should do this more often," Virginia

Williams said. "It has been too long since I've seen all of you."

Violet Colburn nodded in agreement. "That is why I arranged this dinner. We have all been moving in different directions for so long now that I hardly know what you all are up to. My mother asked me how Alice was doing a week ago, and I almost had to ask who she meant."

I gasped. "You could forget me so soon?"

"Never," Violet teased, patting my hand where it rested on the edge of the table. "I remembered you at once, but I didn't have an interesting answer for my mother. So, unfortunately, you have been invited around for afternoon tea sometime this week."

"And unfortunately I will have come down with a sudden illness the moment this meal is over," I said, feigning a cough. "I think it will last a week at least."

"All of you are rotten now," Dorothy said, eyes wide like she'd been scandalized, but her smile showing genuine amusement. "A married woman like me shouldn't be hanging around with you ill mannered single women. People will begin to talk."

"And we'll all still be too busy to hear any of the gossip," Virginia said. She adjusted the white collar of her dress, ensuring it lay flat.

While the rest of us were in slightly different versions of the same evening gown, Virginia wore a dark gray dress in the style of a suit. The shoulders were square with buttons running down the center. And rather than rounded edges to her collar, they came to a point on either side of her neck like a man's dress shirt. It was quite unlike anything else in the entire restaurant. Perhaps, in the whole of London.

"Are you still in classes at the university?" I asked. "Business classes if the rumors I have no time to listen to are true."

"The rumors are true," Virginia said. "I hope to be hired as a buyer. Perhaps by Debenhams or Harrods or the like. With enough luck, I'll work my way up to being a designer."

"You design clothes?" Violet asked. "Why haven't you made me anything fabulous yet?"

Virginia leaned back in her chair. "Because I haven't designed anything yet. I *hope* to be a designer."

"Since meeting Reginald, we have done almost all of our shopping at Marks and Spencer. It is really a nice little store. The dress I'm wearing now is from there, actually." Dorothy held out her arms to illustrate the splendor of her gown, and Virginia concealed a groan.

"I am hoping for something more high end," Virginia said.

Dorothy looked ready to protest, but the waiter came at that very moment to take our drink orders.

Since marrying a police sergeant, Dorothy had shifted from a somewhat aristocratic upbringing to middle-class. It made no difference to me or any of our friends, but everyone believed the adjustment had been less smooth than she let on.

Violet fumbled with the drink menu when it was her turn to order, and after several attempts to flip the menu over, she finally ordered a simple red wine and stared down at her lap. The waiter frowned slightly at Violet's bumbling, looking confused before he rearranged his features and promised to return with our orders soon.

"Our waiter has a fine face," I said, raising an eyebrow at Violet, suspecting that was the source of her nerves.

"I'm certain he does not have the personality to match." Violet shifted in her chair, looking like she needed to stand up and take a turn about the room to work off some of her energy.

"He was fine," Virginia said. "But if you want to find truly handsome men, you should go to the university."

"And men of an appropriate social status," Violet added. "I wouldn't allow that man to take out my help."

"Someone has high standards," I said, nudging Violet. Then, I turned to Virginia. "And I thought you were at the university strictly for your education."

Virginia, unflappable, waved me away. "You think I don't have time for both?"

The conversation veered into the details of each woman's life as our drinks arrived and an hour slipped away. Dorothy spoke of her relief that her baby would be born soon as she didn't want to be heavily expectant in the winter.

"Being cooped up inside all winter sounds miserable, doesn't it? I want to be able to walk and get outside without worrying about slipping and falling on ice."

"So, you would rather be cooped up inside with a newborn all winter?" Virginia asked.

Dorothy thought on that for several minutes, trying to decide which was worse. Several times, I thought she would leave the table altogether, rush home, and discuss the situation with Reginald.

Violet, however, had nothing to add to the matter. She

was the reason we were all at dinner in the first place, but she seemed distracted.

Virginia discussed the perpetual disappointment she was to her parents since she had not paired off with a man yet.

"They expected me to be like my older sister," she said, rolling her eyes. "She is two years older than me and has three children. My father thinks I'm too modern. You must know what I mean, Alice."

I shrugged. "Catherine lived in America for over a year with no immediate plans to return, so my father almost disowned her."

An exaggeration, to be sure, but my father still mentioned frequently that he couldn't believe Catherine even considered settling in America, and he expected my cousin Rose and her husband Achilles to return from there any day now.

"The country isn't even two centuries old," I said, mimicking Papa's voice. "There is no history there. Everything is new and shiny, which is fine for a time, but is no place to raise a family."

"You must be the golden child then," Dorothy said. "You didn't move away or—"

Murder anyone.

Her next words hung silently in the air, waiting to be spoken into existence, but she didn't have to say them for everyone to know what she meant.

Dorothy's face flushed deep crimson, and I smiled, waving away her apology. "I'm sure if I continue on being single any longer my parents will begin to complain, but right now, they are simply happy I am happy."

"That must be nice," Virginia grumbled.

The girls didn't know about my visit to Scotland or the death in Druiminn Castle.

The news had not made its way from Scotland to London yet, and even if it did, no one knew I had travelled there with my mother. It wasn't a secret exactly, just a hastily planned and short trip. And since my mother had been spending her days since the trip in the house and not taking visitors, none of her acquaintances knew of the news, which meant none of mine did, either.

And I had no intention of filling them in.

So, the conversation moved from me to Violet rather quickly.

"You called us all here," Virginia said to her. "How have you been?"

"Good," Violet said, her blue eyes darting around the restaurant as though she was expecting someone.

Virginia shook her head. "I admitted I am a disappointment to my family, Dorothy discussed her upcoming baby, and Alice—well, Alice has been through enough. You have to tell us something worth the cost of dinner, at least."

Occasionally, being the person with the most personal tragedy worked in my favor. Currently, it meant I would avoid an interrogation.

"Are you seeing anyone?" Virginia asked.

"Not presently," Violet said. "I have been working with my mother's charity at the art house. She thinks it could turn into a part-time position for me."

"I wanted to stop in and see a show in there last month," Dorothy said. "We walked past and I tried to convince Reginald, but we were already late for dinner with friends as it was."

"Last month was the modern style portrait exhibit," Violet said. "A really great show. One of the pieces was considered for a prestigious award. No word yet if it has been accepted, but the artist is hopeful."

Virginia feigned a yawn and turned on Violet. "Last time we spoke, you told me you'd met someone. It was all very secretive. Any updates on that?"

Violet blinked and shook her head, looking down at the edge of the tablecloth as though it had suddenly become very interesting. "It wasn't a good match in the end. Nothing much to say."

I could tell Virginia was not done with Violet in the least, but before she could push much harder, a man approached our table.

I recognized him vaguely, though I couldn't say from where. After attending so many different parties and functions, many of the faces became background noise, just passing figures of little importance. This man clearly thought himself important, though.

As he approached our table, he straightened the lapels of his jacket and expanded his chest. His soft chin jutted outward, and he looked down at the tables he passed over a slight bulge in his nose where it looked like it had been broken and not set properly.

Violet was in a position to see the man approach, and she stiffened and took a quick drink of water for seemingly no reason other than to have something to do with her hands. I wondered whether she knew the man, but I didn't have to wonder long.

"Violet," he said, dragging out the vowels in her name to add several unnecessary syllables. "What a surprise running into you here."

"I come here often, actually," she said quietly, giving the man a tight smile.

"I suppose I haven't been here for a while. Not since before I left for Lincoln in Oxford, which was years ago now."

The man tossed his head to the side, his small tuft of brown hair flopping limply to one side, and looked around the table with a smile. After several uncomfortable seconds of silence, it became clear he had no intention of introducing himself.

"Ladies, this is Giles Burton," Violet said grudgingly.

"We've met," Virginia said, eyes narrowed.

Giles paled slightly at the sight of Virginia and shifted himself away from her. "Yes, we are acquainted. In fact, I recognize several of you from various events around the city. Even in a city this large, it is hard to escape one's peers."

Violet rolled her eyes and looked down at her lap.

"It has been several months since I've heard anything from you," Giles said to Violet. He lowered his voice as though the conversation was private, but it was obvious everyone could hear him. "Have there been any notable changes in your situation?"

Virginia's eyebrow raised in question. *What situation?*

"No," Violet said sharply. "None whatsoever. My life is the same as ever. Nothing to report. I wish everyone would leave it alone already."

Giles pulled back slightly, seemingly surprised at Violet's sudden outburst. His expression was mimicked in the faces of our less observant friends around the table who had not been paying attention to Violet's slow build of frustration. As if to hide his embarrassment, he turned towards Dorothy.

"Now, forgive me if I'm mistaken, but you were married last year, yes?"

Dorothy nodded enthusiastically. "Did you see the announcement in the paper? My mother insisted on it being large so no one would miss the news."

"Then she succeeded," Giles said. "Now, remind me of your husband's name?"

"Sergeant Reginald Thompson," she said with a smile.

Giles Burton furrowed his brow and shook his head. "No, I'm sorry. I must not be acquainted with him."

Dorothy's smile dimmed. "He is a...sergeant. With the police."

Giles smiled kindly. "I hope to meet him one day."

"I'm sure you will," Dorothy said, sitting taller. "He is a very well-known man around the city."

That was true, but mostly because Dorothy insisted it was so. She met Sergeant Reginald Thompson at a dance she attended with one of her cousins purely as a favor. The scene was not typical for girls of Dorothy's class, and I remembered her protesting that she had to go at all. *If it was anyone other than Emma, I would say no. But she is dear to me and wants to meet a man and those dances are the only real chance she has, so I'm going with her. If all goes well, I'll be able to sneak out after the first slow dance.*

Then, she met the handsome sergeant and the rest was a whirlwind romance ending in a small wedding. Dorothy was still adjusting to her new station as a middle-class housewife, and probably would be for the remainder of her life.

Giles then turned his attention to me. I smiled stiffly, hoping I could stave him off with quiet politeness, but he leaned forward, eyebrow arched. "And you are?"

"Alice Beckingham," I said, holding out a hand.

He took it and made to kiss my knuckles over the table, but I pulled away before his lips could make contact.

"Alice Beckingham," he repeated, awareness obviously flooding through him all at once. "Your family—"

"Kept the local papers in business a few years back," I finished for him, sounding just as bitter as I felt. "Yes, you've heard of me."

Virginia stifled a laugh, and I didn't feel the usual rush of guilt that commonly accompanied one of my outbursts. It seemed to me, based on the reactions of both Violet and Virginia to the man's presence, that Giles Burton was in desperate need of some rejection.

"I see," he said warmly, nostrils flared. Then, he walked around the table to Violet, leaning down to grab her hand in his. "Hopefully we will run into one another again. It is always a pleasure to see you."

"Yes," Violet said, not sounding at all convincing. She pulled her hand from him gently, but with obvious displeasure at the touch. "Always a pleasure."

Giles Burton turned to leave but was stopped by our waiter, who smiled warmly. "Will you be staying?"

"No," Giles said, wrinkling his nose in distaste at having to speak with the help. "I will not be."

The waiter bowed slightly and then moved clockwise around the table, refreshing our drinks. "Are you all ready to place your orders? The special tonight is roast grouse with stewed fruits."

Virginia and I both ordered the special, while Dorothy opted for the house stew without asking the evening's flavor. When it came to Violet's turn, she stood up and grabbed my arm. "I actually need to use the powder room. To freshen up. Could you come with me, Alice?"

"Yes," I said curiously, "but why don't you order first?"

She looked at the waiter with obvious frustration, bothered at being delayed, and then nodded. "I'll have the same."

"The special or the stew?" he asked.

"The special," Violet said, eyes downturned toward the floor. "Please."

The man nodded, glancing around the table to try and figure out whether he had interrupted at a bad time. The rest of us were wondering the same thing.

"Is everything all right, Violet?" Dorothy asked when he left. "You seem nervous. Was it that man who came over to talk with us? He was self-important, wasn't he? I wouldn't doubt if he really did know Reginald all along, but said he didn't just to make me feel small. I've learned there are a lot of men like that."

"I'm fine," Violet said, taking a drink. "I just want to freshen up."

"All right." I grabbed her hand and moved to stand up. "We can go to the ladies room together."

I could tell Violet had something to tell me. She and I had never been especially close. Virginia had always been her confidante, which was probably why she was the most anxious to get more information out of Violet concerning her personal life. But for whatever reason, Violet wanted to speak to me, and I was happy to oblige.

Violet looked as though a weight lifted from her shoulders as she stood up. As though simply sitting at the table required a great deal of effort.

Just as I was turning around, a gentle hand touched my shoulder.

"Alice Beckingham."

I looked and saw an older couple standing behind me. The woman had rouged cheeks and smiled at me warmly. She was standing so closely that I had to lean back before I could take in the entire picture and recognize her as an old friend of my cousin Rose.

"Mrs. Worthing."

She nodded, pleased I remembered her. "It is so wonderful to see you, Alice. It has been—years. Oh my, years. Can you believe that, Mr. Worthing?"

"I can't," the man said, smiling over his wife's shoulder. "Retirement makes the days and weeks and months blur together."

"And we've been travelling," Mrs. Worthing said. "Nowhere far or fabulous the way Rose did, but we've made our way to all of the nearby sights. We saw the White Cliffs of Dover last month."

Violet dropped down in her seat again with a sigh, and I let go of my clutch, letting it fall back in my chair. If I remembered anything about the Worthings, Mrs. Worthing would be talking for quite some time.

"Have you spoken with Rose recently?" she asked. "San Francisco, is that right?"

"That is right," I said. "She and Achilles moved there right after their wedding."

"Oh, and what a beautiful wedding it was," she said, dreamy-eyed.

"You were there?" I asked. "The day was so busy I could hardly keep track of myself let alone the guests."

"Yes," she said. "Mr. Worthing and I both count it a blessing to be friends of Rose for so many years now. And to think we were just her chaperones for a couple of weeks. Now, I feel like she is one of my children."

"Grandchild is more like it," Mr. Worthing said.

Mrs. Worthing frowned at the idea that she looked too old to be Rose's mother and then smiled at me. "Rose met Monsieur Prideaux the same week she met us. Did you know that?"

"Yes, she explained the story to me."

"We were there when it all happened," she said, wrapping her arm around her husband's. "I knew from the moment I saw them together that there was a connection there. I am just so happy Rose could find a happy ending for herself. I only wish it didn't have to be so far from us. We do miss her."

"I will be sure to send your love in my next letter," I said. "I'm due to write her back soon."

Mrs. Worthing waved me away. "I can do it, dear. Despite her busy life, Rose remains in close contact with me. We both cherish her every letter. Like I said, we think of her as a daughter."

"I'm glad to hear it," I said, smiling and shifting back towards my table. "Well, I do not want to be rude."

"Of course," Mrs. Worthing said. "We should get going, too. We have old work friends of Mr. Worthing's waiting for us. He hasn't seen them in several years since they just arrived last week from India."

"It is warm in here," Violet said behind me as Mrs. Worthing carried on the one-sided conversation.

"I don't think so," Dorothy said. "I'm almost wishing I'd kept my coat. My arms are chilled."

Violet coughed.

"Maybe you are ill?" Dorothy asked. "Does she have a fever, Virginia?"

"I'm not a doctor," Virginia said. "Do you have a fever, Violet?"

"In India, we all had dinner together once a week, but now it has almost been three years," Mrs. Worthing said with a laugh. "Isn't it funny how time works?"

I nodded in agreement, hoping that by not speaking I could discourage Mrs. Worthing, but if anything, she felt more of a need to fill the silence with her voice.

"And you," she said, gesturing to me. "You were just a girl the first time I met you, and now you are a woman. So beautiful."

"Thank you. And you have hardly changed," I said. This was not a lie because I only vaguely remembered what Mrs. Worthing looked like the first time I'd met her.

"I think I need some air," Violet said suddenly, shoving her chair away from the table, knocking the leg of mine.

My chair hit me in the back of the leg, and I stumbled forward and had to catch myself on Mrs. Worthing who shrieked as though I had tried to attack her.

"I'm sorry," Violet and I both said at the same time.

I turned around and realized that Violet looked violet. She was beyond pale. Her skin had taken on a blueish undertone, and her eyes were wide.

"Are you all right?" I asked, forgetting about Mrs. Worthing for a moment.

Violet started to nod her head, but the small amount

of movement caused her to lose her balance. All at once, she dropped to her knees and then tipped forward onto her chair.

Mrs. Worthing shouted again, and I wanted to turn and tell the woman to be quiet. She was drawing too much attention. When Violet woke up from fainting, she would be embarrassed.

But then, the arm Violet had dangling over the top of her chair began to shake, and it took me a moment to recognize that her entire body was shaking. She was convulsing.

3

V iolet slid from the chair to the floor as the patrons around us began to stand up.

Virginia screamed for a doctor and Dorothy rushed around the table to help me roll Violet to her back.

Violet thrashed on the floor, her eyes rolling back in her head and her lips trembling. I desperately wished I had the coolness under pressure that Rose had. I felt useless. Utterly useless.

"Protect her head," Virginia said, pointing to the table leg.

I pushed the chairs away, clearing an area so Violet wouldn't hurt herself.

"Does she have any kind of condition?" the waiter asked, kneeling down next to me.

His eyes were wide and his face pale, but he reached out and pinned Violet's arms to her sides.

"A doctor has been sent for," he said. "But if there is

anything we can do before then. Any medication she is on?"

"Nothing," Dorothy said. She turned to me. "Right?"

"I don't think so," I said.

"Not that I know of," Virginia said, clapping a hand over her mouth and looking down at our friend. "She has always been healthy. This has never happened before."

I didn't look around to see where Mr. or Mrs. Worthing had gone. I barely registered anyone else in the restaurant at all. The entire room had narrowed to Violet lying on the floor.

She'd been hot and out of breath. When she'd turned to me, her face had been pale.

All evening she had been acting strange. Had she been sick and no one had noticed?

She wanted to go to the ladies room and freshen up. If we'd gone—if we hadn't been stopped by Mrs. Worthing —would she be all right now?

I pushed such thoughts from my mind, trying to save my energy for more useful things. Like taking care of Violet.

Suddenly, the thrashing stopped.

I pulled my hands away from her head and stared down at her, waiting for her to open her eyes. To explain what this was and why it had happened.

Maybe Violet had been keeping a secret medical condition from us. Maybe that was why she'd called this sudden dinner after so many months apart. It seemed an unusual thing to do, but everything about tonight seemed unusual, so I could no longer judge.

"Is she breathing?" Dorothy asked, squinting down at her.

"Of course, she is," I said before she could even get the question out. "It was a convulsive fit. Just a fit."

My heart hammered against my rib cage. Where was the doctor? When would he arrive?

The waiter reached out slowly and pressed his fingers to Violet's neck. Then, he pulled them back quickly as though she was hot to the touch.

His expression was the only answer I needed.

"She isn't breathing," Dorothy said softly, her words both a question and a statement.

Virginia dropped down into her chair, a hand over her face, and I fell back, staring at the lifeless body in front of me.

She'd been breathing only moments ago. I'd seen it. I'd felt the thrum of her heart against my palm as I held onto her.

"But it was just a fit," I said. My voice sounded small in the suddenly stifling room.

There was a doctor in the restaurant just next door. He came over when he heard the raucous, but by the time he settled down to examine Violet, it was already too late.

THE NEXT HOUR passed in a blur.

Violet's body was carried away by the police. They laid her on a stretcher, covered her with a black blanket, and loaded her into the back of a waiting car.

It felt wrong to let her go alone. I wanted to go after her and ride in the back, ensure they treated her with the respect she deserved.

But if they didn't, Violet wouldn't know the difference. She was dead.

"I can't believe it," Dorothy sobbed, wiping her face with the cloth napkin that had been meant for our dinner. "She was fine. Perfectly fine. And then…"

"Well," I said, shrugging. "I'm not sure she was fine. She was acting strangely, wasn't she?"

Virginia and Dorothy both furrowed their brows in confusion, but before they could give voice to their doubts, a police officer sat down in the chair that had been Violet's.

"Hello, ladies. I am sorry about your loss, but I'm here to talk to you about the events of tonight." The man was large, his voice was deep, and none of us knew exactly how to respond to him. His matter of fact manner of speaking felt cold in the face of what we'd experienced.

Dorothy immediately burst into another bout of tears and Virginia just stared ahead at the far wall.

The restaurant had been emptied of people except for the wait staff and our table.

Our waiter continued bringing us drinks and even offered to bring us our dinners, though we had all more than lost our appetites. Besides, I knew if I ate that grouse, I would never be able to eat grouse again without thinking of Violet. And I rather liked grouse.

"Now, did you notice anything unusual about your friend's behavior tonight?" he asked. "Did she say anything out of the ordinary? Anything that alarmed you?"

Dorothy shook her head, dabbing at her dripping nose with her napkin. "I do not think so. Though, Alice was just saying she thought Violet was acting strangely."

"And Violet is the deceased?" the detective asked, turning towards me.

"Yes. She was our friend," I said rather defensively.

He pressed his lips together and made note of something in a small notepad that was clutched in his meaty hand. "And you said she was acting strangely?"

"Nervous," I said simply. "She seemed slightly out of sorts. Just before she fell over, she asked me to go to the powder room with her."

"That could have been because she didn't feel well," Virginia said.

"I know," I said. "All of her behavior tonight could have been because she did not feel well. It is just that—well, she seemed nervous all night. That is all I noticed."

"Nervous," the detective said, writing it down. "Do you know of any reason why she would be nervous?"

We all agreed that we had no idea. The dinner was supposed to be an evening for all of us to catch up and see what each other was up to. Had the dinner continued as planned, I might have learned a vital piece of information from Violet. As it was, none of us learned anything.

The questioning continued for several more minutes, but none of us had anything of value to add to the investigation. When the detective realized this, he once again expressed his sympathy for our loss and then dismissed us.

So, huddled and unsure, we stood outside the restaurant staring at one another.

"It feels wrong to leave," Virginia said. "We shouldn't be leaving without her."

"Do you think all of this will make more sense when we wake up tomorrow?" Dorothy asked.

"I'm not sure," I admitted. I could have taken that opportunity to tell them about the death at Druiminn Castle. Or Edward's. I could have explained to them how I had dealt with sudden deaths in the past.

But I didn't want to frighten them.

Silly as it sounded, I was also frightened myself. What would they think if I relayed to them the long list of people who had died in my presence? Would they turn around and inform the police that I should be the main suspect?

I was too overwhelmed by everything to know whether I was being foolish or not, so I decided to say nothing.

Dorothy shook her head. "This doesn't feel real."

Suddenly, a man in a dark blue suit with a thick curled mustache rushed toward us. I jumped in surprise, but then Dorothy let out a wailing kind of sob.

"Reginald." She folded herself into the man's arms, and Virginia and I both looked at one another.

It would have been nice to collapse into someone right then.

George pulled up along the curb in the car and then got out to stand by the front bumper, waiting for me. I nodded to let him know I saw him and then turned back to Virginia.

"Will the police let us know what happened? What... caused all of this?" I asked.

"Reginald will make sure of it," Dorothy said, wiping at her eyes, her cheek pressed against her husband's chest. "Won't you, Reg?"

He assured us all that we would know the most pertinent information as soon as he did. That was all that was left to be done. So, with a flimsy wave, I stumbled towards the car and rode home.

THE NEWS FELT SO momentous that I expected for the information to have reached everyone by now. Yet, when I walked through the front door, my parents were not waiting anxiously in the foyer for me.

The light in my father's study was on, and the sitting room was dark, meaning my mother was upstairs in her room. They were both blissfully unaware of what I had endured.

And for the moment, that was fine. I closed the door behind me and walked quietly to the stairs.

"Alice?" My father's voice was faint, barely making it through the crack in the study door.

"It's me," I said. "I'm home."

My voice sounded strange to my own ears.

He mumbled something, but I didn't catch it, and he didn't repeat himself.

My mother didn't hear me walk down the hallway and into my room, which meant I might be able to make it until morning before I had to tell anyone about what had happened.

I'd seen death before. Plenty of it. And perhaps that was why Violet's death hit me so hard.

It was everywhere.

It happened to my family, other people's families, to strangers. And now to my friends.

I had seen more death in my young life than most people did in a lifetime, and I wasn't entirely sure how to cope with it. Especially when I still didn't know what happened. When there were no answers.

It was better to know someone had been murdered than to know nothing at all.

No, that wasn't true. Well, it was, but it was wrong to say so. I shouldn't wish for Violet to have been murdered.

I threw my purse onto my bed and dropped down on the edge of it, my coat still pulled around my shoulders.

I knew it wouldn't help anything to think about it, but I couldn't help but wonder if I could have done something. If I had pressed to see what was the matter or if I had gone with Violet to the ladies room—could I have saved her?

I flopped back on the bed and sighed.

When I did, however, I heard a crinkle underneath me.

My desire to melt into the mattress was great, but my curiosity won out. I sat up and turned around.

Crumpled on top of my mattress was a folded piece of purple stationery.

I nearly picked it up and threw it on the desk next to my bed, thinking it a letter that had gotten lost in the mail that one of the maids had brought up while I was out. But then I thought it could be a nice distraction from everything. So, I unfolded the letter.

As soon as I saw the handwriting, my heart clenched.

I scanned the short letter to read the sign-off at the end, and a choked sob forced itself out of me.

Violet.

I looked around the room, trying to figure out how the letter had found its way to my bed. I hadn't noticed it before I left, and Violet certainly hadn't sent it to me after dinner, as she was busy on the other side of town in the morgue.

Then, I saw my purse tipped on its side, my small compact and a comb sliding out of it.

The letter must have fallen out of my purse when I'd thrown it on the bed, which meant Violet must have dropped it into my purse at some point during the dinner.

I hurried back to the top and read the letter through, not breathing once until I'd finished.

Alice,

I know I could have asked you this question during dinner, but if I am being honest, I am too nervous. I feel silly making such a fuss out of what may be nothing. However, I am fearful enough that I cannot let it go. To put it simply, I believe I am in danger.

The details are scarce and mostly my own conjecturing, but I want to speak to someone. The police will not do anything to help me because there has been no crime committed and the details of the matter are too delicate to be shared amongst the local police, anyway. That being the case, the only person I could think of was your cousin Rose.

Her name was in the papers more than once in the last several years for solving one crime or another, and she married a world famous detective. I'm sure they are rather busy, but I hope you will put me in touch with them. The matter is somewhat urgent, and I am willing to pay them handsomely for their assistance.

Please keep the details of this letter between yourself and your cousin. I do not want anyone to know I am seeking outside assistance on the matter.

Warmly,
     Violet

I READ the note a second time and then a third.

Each time, it was harder to believe I could not go to Violet's house and talk to her about the letter.

Why hadn't I noticed it sooner? If I'd felt her drop it into my bag, I would have read it immediately. I could have talked to her about what details were "too delicate" for the police. I could have understood why this matter was urgent and why she was afraid.

The letter said she was too nervous to speak to me in person about it, but Violet had grabbed my hand at the end of dinner and almost pulled me towards the ladies room. She was forceful. Clearly, she had something to say, and I'd allowed myself to be distracted by Mrs. Worthing.

What information could Violet have imparted in the span of the pointless conversation I'd had with the older woman and her husband? What secrets did I miss out on?

I held the letter in my hand, staring at the impression of the pen on the page, and came to a conclusion.

Violet was murdered.

The body hadn't been properly examined yet and the police didn't know anything, but my instincts told me Violet did not die a natural death.

How could she have? On the same night she dropped this letter into my purse? It was too much of a coincidence.

Violet was afraid, and I now knew she was afraid for her life.

I folded the letter and held it in my hand as I lifted myself from the bed and began pacing across the floor.

I did not have the opportunity to help Violet while she was alive, but I would help her now. I would uncover what or who she was afraid of and why. And I did not need the help of Rose or Achilles to do it.

Rose and Achilles were settled in San Francisco. Bringing them here for a case I had almost no information on seemed selfish, especially since Violet's suspicions could yet turn out to be a misunderstanding.

Besides, I solved the murder in Druiminn Castle when no one thought I could. My mother was still shaken up by the death, but I was not rattled. I remained calm and collected, and I caught the murderer before they could dispose of the evidence or kill someone else.

And I would do the same with this case. I would find justice for Violet.

4

Mama practically threw herself across the breakfast table when I told my parents the news.

I'd done my best to deliver the information delicately. To prepare them for the worst. But still, they were both shocked. Numb for a moment before my mother gasped and began to weep.

"Violet Colburn? Your friend?" she asked, draping her arms across the back of my chair and laying her head on my shoulder. "Why didn't you tell us last night?"

"I heard you come home," my father said, shaking his head. "You sounded fine."

I didn't say much to him when I came home or vice versa. There was no way he could have heard enough from me to know whether I was fine or not. In fact, if he had pried at all, I was weak enough in the moment that I would have cracked. But I did not say any of this at the time. It would only give my parents something to argue about later. Mama felt Papa spent far too much of his time buried in the news and too little of it tending to his family.

"Are you all right?" my mother asked, pulling back from me. "You are not feeling ill, are you?"

"I am fine," I said. "Violet collapsed at dinner. If I was sick, too, I would have died by now."

My mother blanched at the words and turned away, the back of her hand pressed to her mouth. She stood up and paced away from me.

"I should send our condolences to her family at once. It has already been too long."

"That hardly matters," I said.

"It does matter," my mother snapped, shaking her head, her lips trembling. "You were there, Alice. We should have been the first to reach out."

I stood up and moved next to my mother, a hand on her shoulder. She slouched slightly at my touch and sighed.

"I'm fine, Mama. Really."

She laid a hand over mine and nodded. "I know."

I lead her back to her chair and forced her to finish breakfast before writing any letters. Father managed to stay out of his newspaper for a few minutes before he began to creep behind it again.

It was how they each dealt with things after Edward died.

My mother wrote letters and reached out to friends and sent 'thank yous' to those who sent their condolences. And my father buried himself in reading and his study and work. Now, even when the death was outside of our family, their response was the same.

After breakfast, my mother rushed up to get to her

desk, but stopped in the doorway. "What are your plans today, Alice?"

"I'm about to head out for a walk," I said, straightening my skirt and buttoning the bottom two buttons of my sweater.

My mother frowned. "Is that wise?"

"I think so," I said. "I want fresh air and outside is the only place to get it."

Her frown deepened, a line forming between her brows. "I think you should stay indoors for today. You've just endured something dreadful, and I don't want you out alone."

"I am fine, Mama. Truly."

She looked uncertain, but I just smiled and waved. "If I need to have an emotional breakdown, I promise to rush home and have it in front of you. Does that help?"

My mother rolled her eyes and waved me away, swatting lightly at my father's paper as she passed.

Truly, I was fine. Because I had a plan.

Last night, I felt overwhelmed and confused and unprepared. Now, I had a goal.

I would solve Violet's murder.

I could not tell my mother that, though. She thought Violet had died of a mysterious illness. The moment she learned it was murder, she would do her best to lock me inside and never let me leave again.

Never mind the fact Violet and I had very few acquaintances in common. Aside from Dorothy and Virginia, we hardly moved in the same circles. The dinner was the first time I had even seen Violet face to face in almost two years. It had been a surprise invitation, though welcomed, and now I suspected she had only invited me to gain a connection to Rose and Achilles.

Still, I was not bitter. Even if her intention had not been to ask me for my help, Violet would get my help. I simply needed to find myself a reliable assistant.

～

GEORGE LIVED in a small building behind the main house, where he kept a close watch on the family car. As I walked across the yard towards his home, I realized I had never been inside.

For as long as I could remember, George lived back there, quietly keeping to himself, coming and going when he wasn't driving for us. There just never seemed a reason or opportunity to explore the space. Even during a short period when George had moved out—by force since he had been dismissed due to a misunderstanding in which my parents thought he could be a dangerous criminal—Edward told me scary stories about being murdered if I ever went into the chauffeur's living quarters. So, I kept my distance.

That was why it felt so strange to be standing in front of the door and waiting for George to answer my knock. A light drizzle had been falling from the sky all morning, but it had thankfully cleared, allowing me to wait without getting wet.

When he did come to the door, George's eyes went wide with surprise, though he quickly tried to hide it.

"Miss Alice," he said, tipping his head. "To what do I owe the pleasure? Is there anything I can do for you?"

"Hello, George." I smiled. "Actually, I hoped to step inside and speak with you. If you have a moment."

That sentence contained the most words I had ever spoken to the man consecutively.

His brow furrowed in either confusion or curiosity, but he stepped aside and welcomed me indoors.

The space was small, but tidy. There was a kitchen area in the back corner with a small table and two chairs against the wall. I wondered if George ever had guests back here. Surely he did, though I had never seen any of them come or go. In the front was a small sofa set before a stove with a single lamp next to it. The windows were open to allow in the morning light. Overall, the room looked comfortable.

George closed the door and stood next to it, seeming nervous about following me into the room.

I knew it wasn't entirely appropriate for me to be alone with him in this setting. My mother, while trusting of George these days, would surely reprimand me if she knew I was here. But some things were more important than propriety.

"What is it you wanted to discuss, Miss Alice?" he asked, folding his hands behind his back.

I swung my hands nervously at my sides before following George's lead and folding them together behind my back. There seemed to be no better way to approach the subject than to dive right in. "You briefly worked for my cousin Rose while she lived in London. When she did not live in my family's house, I mean."

"I did," he said. "She hired me when...well, I'm sure you remember. You were young, but old enough—"

"Yes, I remember," I finished for him, hoping to avoid

any conversation of his being unfairly dismissed, even though the matter had been corrected in the end. "You worked for her in a larger capacity than just as a driver, correct?"

George ran a hand across his mouth and tilted his head to the side. "I'm not sure I entirely understand the question."

I let out a breath. "Rose acted as a private detective and solved mysteries. Murders, most notably. And you helped, is that right?"

He opened and closed his mouth several times, clearly too nervous to continue.

"This is not an interrogation," I said, hoping to quell his fears. "My parents do not know I am here, and I am not trying to get you in trouble. I am only curious."

"Your parents do not know?" he asked, looking over his shoulder as though they could see us through the walls. "Well, then, I'm not sure—"

"Should they be displeased, I will take full responsibility," I said. "Now, please, could you answer the question?"

George stepped away from the wall slightly, still leaving a large gap between the two of us, and then nodded. "I helped Miss Rose when I could. She occasionally put herself in dangerous situations, and I felt it was my duty to look out for her."

"That was very gentlemanly of you," I said, warmly.

I didn't know what to say next. In my head, I had prepared an argument for why George should help me, but now it all seemed flimsy. This was the longest conversation we had ever had. He worked for my family, but he did not know me. Not really. He had no obligation or connection to me, and I was asking him to possibly risk his position with my family. It all seemed very selfish now that I was standing in front of him. Childish, even.

"Is that all you needed?" George asked, confused.

"No," I said quickly. "Well, I suppose I should start at the beginning. My friend died last night."

George nodded. "I recall. I am sorry for your loss."

"Oh, right. I nearly forgot you picked me up," I said, shaking my head. "Clearly, I am out of sorts."

"To be expected," he said.

"You are too understanding, George. Well, then there seems to be no need to start at the beginning. You know that bit. I will move on: I believe my friend was murdered."

His eyes widened, and he stepped forward. "Why do you say that? Are you in trouble, Miss?"

"Oh, no," I said quickly. "At least, I do not believe so. Violet seems to have been the sole target. But I am interested in attempting to solve her killing."

"Pardon me for saying so, but surely that would be a job for the police, Miss Alice? Miss Rose...well, she was a particular sort of person. She had a gift for these kinds of things. Not to say you do not. It is just—well—"

"I am not a child," I said sharply. "My friend left a letter in my purse before she died. She was asking me for help, and I intend to give it."

That was a lie. A small one. Violet wanted my help connecting her to Rose, but that did not matter. George did not need to know.

"The police do not know this was a murder yet, and I want to find proof that it was. I hoped you would assist me in the same way you helped Rose."

I did not know the ways in which George helped
Rose, but I was desperate for any assistance I could get.
Even being driven around town without any questions or
fear word would get back to my parents could be helpful.
Though I was an adult, they still felt the need to monitor
my movements rather closely. I needed to be able to
investigate without their notice.

"I hope I did not offend you," George said, looking
down at the floor between us. "I just do not want to see
you put yourself in harm's way."

"I won't," I said.

The silence between us grew. I had admitted my plan
to George, and if he wished to do so, he could walk right
past me into the main house and tell my parents everything. And despite my proclamation that I was an adult
who would do as I wished, their disapproval would be a
large obstacle to overcome.

"What help would you require from me?" he asked. "I
am already your driver, so I will continue to do that
regardless of where you ask me to take you."

I bit my lip. "There are people I may need to speak
with who are difficult to locate. Is that something you did
for Rose?"

"I am willing to try," he said, sounding slightly
unsure. Though, I would have been more suspicious if he
had been enthusiastic. What I was asking him to do was
not part of his job description and could get him into
trouble. He had a right to be nervous.

"Can we sit?" I asked, pointing towards the kitchen
table. "We have a lot more to discuss if we are going to be
partners."

"Partners," he said, testing the word. "I would prefer if

you took the lead, and I simply offered my services. Though I have involved myself with other cases, I do not have a particular interest in making this a full-time affair."

"Understood."

We nodded at one another, and then George moved to the table, pulling out a seat for me and then taking his own.

I paraphrased the letter Violet had left in my bag and then walked through the evening's events as far as I could remember them.

"So, you believe someone at the restaurant killed her?" he asked.

"I think so," I said. "Or she was poisoned before she arrived. That is another possibility."

"Poison." George shook his head. "Such a cruel way for a young woman to die."

The image of Violet convulsing on the floor in front of me, her eyes rolled back in her head, flashed in my mind, and I quickly pushed it aside.

"If she was poisoned, then everyone at the table is a suspect. I do not want to consider that one of my friends could have committed the crime, but no one can be ruled out. Also, everyone at the restaurant is a suspect. One person in particular stands out, but I do not know him. It was the first time we had ever met."

Giles Burton stopped by the table briefly, and Violet was made deeply uncomfortable by his presence. At the time, I thought it was because he was insufferable and pompous. Now, however, I had to look at his visit with new eyes. He had stood behind Violet at one point, close enough he could have put something in her drink. If he was clever enough, he could have done so without anyone noticing.

"If you know his name, then I'm sure he can be located," George said.

"I do. It is Giles Burton. The problem is that I have no reason to contact him, and even if I did, I have no reason to believe he would speak with or meet me," I said. "But I do know someone who may have a stronger connection with him. Sherborne Sharp."

George's brow furrowed, and then recognition crossed his face. "You met him in Scotland, correct? I heard your mother mention his name."

"Yes, but he is from London. I recall Mr. Burton mentioning at the restaurant that he attended Lincoln College in Oxford and I know Mr. Sharp attended the same school. His Oxford days were spoken of while we were both guests of the Drummonds in Scotland. Mr. Burton and Mr. Sharp are of a similar age, so they may know one another. The problem is that I do not have a way to contact Sherborne Sharp."

"And you would like me to locate him?" George asked.

"If possible, yes."

"Is there anything I should know about the man before I begin looking for him?" George asked.

He is a thief was the first thing that popped into my mind, but I did not want to give George a reason to back out of the agreement before we had even begun. If he knew I was associating with a criminal crowd from the onset, he might change his mind and report my actions to my parents at once.

"Nothing noteworthy," I said. "If you could just track

him down for me, then I will speak with him. You won't need to make contact."

Mostly because I was afraid Sherborne would disappear if he knew I was looking for him. When we were both guests at the Drummand's castle, I had caught him in a rather compromising position, attempting to steal jewelry from my mother's bedroom, so he would probably not look kindly on me tracking him down. Especially since I planned to use his almost theft as a small encouragement. If he feared I would tell his secrets to the high society friends he was no doubt stealing from, he might be more willing to help me get in touch with Giles Burton.

"All right. Would you like me to start looking for Sherborne Sharp soon?"

"As soon as possible," I admitted. "I need to speak with him before I can move forward with the investigation."

George sighed and pushed himself to standing. "I suppose there is no time like the present then. I have a few contacts I can reach out to. I'll be in touch when I know something."

"Thank you, George," I said sincerely. "And I'm sure you understand this is a delicate matter and—"

"I will not mention it to your parents," he said, giving me a tight-lipped smile.

I thanked him again and left. When I got up to my bedroom and looked out the window, I saw George exit through the back door of his home, get into the car, and drive away.

5

I do not know exactly how long I imagined it would take George to track Sherborne Sharp down, but I expected it to take longer than two hours.

George sent me a note before lunch, letting me know he had found the man and was ready to take me to him as soon as possible.

Quickly, I dressed in a matching rose-colored skirt and jacket with brown oxfords and a cream cloche hat pulled low over my brown curls, which had gone slightly frizzy from the early morning rain.

"Where are you off to?" My mother called from her room as I shut my bedroom door. "Lunch will be soon."

"I'm actually going out for lunch," I called back to her.

Immediately, she poked her head out of her door. "Are you sure? It just seems so soon and—?"

"I cannot help that something horrible happened to my friend," I said. "But I can help how I respond to it. Violet would not want me to hide away in the house on her behalf."

Hurt crossed my mother's face, and I realized how pointed my words sounded. She had scarcely left the house since returning to London except to stand in the back garden for a few minutes every day.

"All right," she said reluctantly. "But be careful. And have George take you wherever you want to go. Your father and I will not need the car."

"I will." I smiled and waved before almost running down the stairs and through the front door. My father was not likely to stop me, but he might feel guilty about not stopping me the night before when I'd come home after the death of my friend, and I did not want him to make up for it now. There was no time.

As soon as he had helped me into the car, George climbed back into the front seat and began to drive. "I have a friend who works for a family whose son is acquaintances with Sherborne Sharp. I drove by the address an hour ago, and he was home. Would you like me to take you there?"

"Yes, please."

The rest of the ride was spent in silence, trying to figure out what exactly I would say. The closer we got, the more my stomach filled with butterflies.

What if Sherborne turned me away? What if he didn't respond to my blackmail?

I could always reach out to Giles Burton on my own, but part of the reason I wanted to make his acquaintance through Sherborne was because I was afraid.

What if Giles had killed Violet? Would he be suspicious that I had looked him up after our very brief encounter at the restaurant? Especially since the encounter had not even been particularly friendly. Would he attack me unprovoked to keep his secret?

My heart began to flutter along with my stomach, and I took a deep breath to calm down. I was getting ahead of myself. I would worry about what to do without Sherborne's help after he refused me. Hopefully, he wouldn't.

George parked the car along a shallow curb. "This is the place."

I'd been so lost in my own thoughts and worries that I hadn't realized where we were.

The neighborhood was far from my family's home and far from any neighborhood where any of my friends lived. I had never been there before and there was good reason.

Sherborne Sharp, despite his clean-cut appearance, refined tastes, and impressive background, lived in squalor.

The buildings were dingy and crumbling with litter clogging the curbs and boards covering the windows. Everything seemed grayer here. Leaving the house, I'd been surprised at how the day had cleared after the morning's rain, but suddenly everything felt cloudy again.

He had told me at Druiminn Castle that he had fallen on hard times. That his thievery came from desperation, and I'd counted it as nothing more than an attempt to force me into pity so I would not tell his secret. Now, however, I wondered whether it wasn't true.

"His flat is on the first floor. There," George said, pointing to a door on the corner. There was a potted plant on the stone steps that had long ago withered and died, leaving nothing but a pile of dirt and sticks behind. "Would you like me to come with you, Miss?"

"No," I said, doubting my answer as soon as I'd said it. "Your presence might make him nervous. But please wait for me here."

"I will," he said. "Good luck."

I wasn't ready to get out of the car yet, but staying felt cowardly. George had wished me luck, and if I hesitated, he would question my ability to handle this business on my own. He no doubt already had reservations about me solving a murder, and I did not want to give him another reason to compare me to Rose and find me lacking. Rose was brave and fearless. I was brave and fearless, too. I just had to prove it to George. And myself.

I got out of the car and stopped briefly on the sidewalk to adjust my skirt and jacket. I was more than a little aware of how much I stood out in this neighborhood in my pink walking skirt. Had I known where I was headed, I would have worn something in a less vibrant shade.

To my left, someone pulled back the edge of a curtain and peered out at me. It was too dark to see their face, but I saw a hand and the dark shape of a body and it was enough to propel me forward. I would rather face Sherborne than wait for one of his neighbors to find me.

His door had water stains around the top and dripping down from the handle in a long shape like an icicle. Leaves and debris were gathered on the steps, in desperate need of sweeping, and I had to be careful knocking to avoid the spiderwebs that covered most of the face of the door.

I expected to have a moment after knocking to gather

myself, but the door opened almost immediately, and standing in front of me was Sherborne Sharp.

He looked just as I remembered him: tall, hair and thin mustache black as pitch, and a handsome face with sharp features. Everything about him seemed balanced and poised, which made it even more difficult to imagine him living in a place like this. It had been difficult before, but now that I was reminded of how he held himself, it didn't make any sense at all.

He took a step back as though I was a ghost before he gathered himself. "Alice Beckingham."

"Sherborne Sharp," I said, hoping I sounded more confident than I felt.

We stared at one another, each waiting for the other to speak, and when it became clear he would say nothing, I started. "Lovely neighborhood."

The small smile he'd managed to feign slipped away. "I'm surprised you even got out of the car. You do not strike me as a woman comfortable among the lower classes."

"Are you calling me a snob?" I asked.

"Are you suggesting you aren't one?" he challenged, placing a hand on his doorframe, making it fully apparent he had no intention of inviting me inside.

I decided to concede. "I did not come here to debate my feelings towards differing social classes."

"Why did you come here?" He looked past me, glancing up and down the street. His eyes paused on the car idling a short distance down the road, but otherwise he seemed comforted.

"For your help."

He choked out a surprised laugh and then narrowed his eyes when I didn't say anything. "You are serious? What could I possibly help you with? Last I knew, you wanted me to keep a very far distance from you and your family."

"Well, you were attempting to steal from my family. What was I supposed to do? Ask you round for lunch?"

He shrugged one shoulder. "That would be nice, actually. My silver set is short a few spoons."

I scowled at him, which only provided him with more amusement. "You are not in the mood for jokes today, either."

A soft roll of thunder sounded in the distance, and I looked up at the clouds, which seemed to be growing darker by the second. I couldn't delay much longer or I would get soaked.

"I came to ask about one of your Oxford peers. Giles Burton."

Sherborne raised an eyebrow and tilted his head. "*You want to speak with Giles Burton? Why?*"

"I take it you know him, then?" It was clear by the look of distaste on his face that he did. I'd worn the same expression after meeting Mr. Burton.

"I do, which is why I'm perplexed why anyone would seek him out willingly," he said. "Giles is not exactly pleasant company."

"And you consider yourself an authority on that subject?" I said before I could think better of it. I sighed. "I'm sorry. I am not here to insult you."

"You could have fooled me," Sherborne said. He crossed his arms over his chest and leaned a shoulder against the door frame. "You said you need my help. With Giles?"

"Yes. I was hoping you could put me in touch with him."

Sherborne stood up tall and placed his hand on the door, beginning to close it as he answered. "No, sorry. He and I haven't been in touch since Oxford. Thank you for visiting, though. We should do this again."

I stepped forward and stopped the door with my hand. "Can you get in touch with him?"

Sherborne shifted his gaze to where my hand was holding the door open, and I could tell he had half a mind to shove my hand out of the way and slam the door. He didn't, though. He opened it again and sighed with obvious annoyance. "I could, but I am not at all convinced that I should."

I took a step back and spent a long moment studying the front of his building and the surrounding ones. What little grass there was had turned brown months ago and everyone I saw wore faded, stained clothing and worn work shoes. Sherborne did not fit in here.

"Apparently, you were not lying about hitting hard times," I said. "That is what you told me in Scotland, remember? That you were stealing from my mother out of desperation."

He pursed his lips together. "Yes, I recall."

"I doubted you at the time, but now your story has significantly more truth to it."

"What does that have to do with anything?" he snapped.

I stepped forward, voice low. "It would be a shame if

word of your hobby made it around to your wealthier friends, wouldn't it? Who would you steal from if you weren't welcomed into their homes and invited to their parties?"

His eyes narrowed further, dark brows furrowed. "I did not take you for a woman capable of blackmail."

"It seems you have underestimated me then," I said with a polite smile. I took a deep breath and clapped my hands together. "Now, I hoped you would reach out to your old friend and reconnect. I have some questions for him."

Sherborne bit his lower lip and stared out at the street. "Do I at least get to know why?"

"He might be a murderer."

His attention snapped back to me, and he stared for a few seconds, making sure I was telling the truth. When he realized I was, he stepped out of the doorway and gestured for me to come inside. "Would you like to come in?"

"No, thank you." The thunder was closer now and the air felt thick with moisture, but I did not want to go into Sherborne's flat yet. I needed his help, but I was under no obligation to trust him. "We don't have anything left to discuss at the moment."

"I disagree," he huffed. "You just told me one of my old classmates might be a murderer. I think that deserves a conversation."

"Which we will have when you are able to put me in touch with him."

Anger bristled off of him, but rather than fear, I felt exhilarated. Sherborne Sharp was, for the time being, under my control. I could see it in the shift of his posture and the look in his eyes. He desperately wanted to know what I was talking about. He wanted to know more, but I was holding back.

The look in his eyes shifted back to bored amusement in an instant, however, and he once again leaned against the doorframe, doing his best to look relaxed. "I thought we were friends, Alice. You do not need to blackmail me."

"Then you were mistaken," I said. I handed him a slip of paper with my information on it. "Get in touch when you can put me in contact with Giles Burton. And, of course, be discreet. I do not want him catching on. As a professional thief, I'm sure you can manage that."

Sherborne was still reading the note when I turned and walked away. I didn't look back, but I could feel his eyes on me as I got in the car and George drove away.

Truthfully, I did feel bad about blackmailing him. Not because Sherborne didn't deserve it, but because as he said, I was not usually the type of person to blackmail anyone. I would much prefer if we were friends, but that seemed unlikely. So, I did what I had to do to get justice for Violet. Including reaching out to a man I despised.

Except, as I thought more on our interaction and the mission I had given Sherborne, I couldn't stop myself from looking forward to our next conversation.

Unlike so many people in my life, Sherborne did not handle me with kid gloves. He treated me as he would anyone else, and while his treatment involved dealing with verbal barbs, it meant he viewed me as an adult.

And that was the reason I gave to the strange feeling I got when I saw him standing in his doorway. It was not that I liked his company. It was simply that in his company, I felt mature. I felt confident.

It had nothing to do with his shiny black hair and angular chin.

6

George dropped me off in front of the house just as he would normally and then drove around. The rain had picked up again, so he got out with an umbrella first to lead me inside. I had my head down to avoid the rain, so I did not immediately notice the police cars parked along the curb. George had to point them out to me.

"Do you think they are here in regards to your friend?" he asked.

"I don't know what else it could be," I said. I thanked him for seeing me to the door. "I will tell you if there is anything worth knowing."

He nodded and turned away before hesitating. "Miss Alice?"

I brushed rain from the front of my jacket. "Yes?"

"I know you will do what you feel is best, but I cannot leave without encouraging you to tell the police what you know."

"I will not lie to them," I said. I might not give them

every piece of evidence I had—the letter was safely locked away in my bedside drawer—but I would tell them what I knew.

George seemed moderately comforted, tipped his head, and then jogged across the sidewalk and back to the car.

As soon as I walked inside, I heard voices in the sitting room. My father had his company voice on. It was a loud, booming voice he used only when other people beyond our family were in the house. It made him seem much more warm and friendly than he usually was.

He was speaking so loudly that no one heard me enter. My mother only noticed my arrival when I took off my hat and shook out my curls in the doorway to the sitting room.

"There she is," my mother said, standing up and rushing over to usher me into the room. She wrapped an arm around my waist. "These detectives have come to speak with you. They nearly left, but I assured them you would be home soon."

"I'm glad I didn't miss you." I smiled to each of the men. I did not recognize them from the restaurant the night before, but I had been very distracted. I could have spoken to one of them directly and not remembered them.

"As are we," one of the detectives said. He was a young man with blonde hair and a matching mustache. He looked scarcely older than I was, though I knew that couldn't be true. A man that young would be giving parking tickets, not working a murder investigation.

His partner was much more what I expected when I thought of a detective. He had gray hair that stuck out from beneath his cap and lines around his mouth and eyes, regardless of whether he was smiling or not. At the moment, he was not smiling. In fact, he was scowling.

"We just wanted to speak with you again about the events of last night," the older detective said. The name plate affixed to his shirt said 'Williams.'

The younger detective—name 'Harrison'—gestured for me to take a seat. Once I did, one parent on either side of me, the detectives sat down on the sofa across from me.

"We know you gave your statement last night," Detective Harrison said. "But it was a chaotic scene and there may have been something important you omitted. By accident, of course."

"Of course," I said, nodding. "I am open to answering any questions. Whatever I can do to help."

My mother smoothed a hand down my back. "It is horrible what happened. Do you know what caused it yet? An illness? Should we be worried?"

The young detective looked to his older partner for guidance, and Detective Williams adjusted his belt and leaned forward, one elbow planted on his knee. "I cannot say whether you should be nervous or not, but we do believe we have a cause of death."

He paused, either for dramatic effect or because he could not read the anticipation in the room.

"Our preliminary investigation leads us to believe Miss Colburn was murdered," he said stoically. "By way of poison."

My mother gasped and slapped a hand over her mouth. "You can't be serious."

"I'm afraid so," Detective Williams said. He turned to

me. "Which is why it is vital we get every detail you have of the night's events."

"Of course," I said softly. "Anything."

My mother was clearly shaken by the news and even my father sat in a dazed silence. So as not to arouse suspicion, I did my best to look surprised, but I'd suspected this possibility over sixteen hours prior.

Slowly, I walked them through the entire evening, from the moment I walked through the restaurant door until the moment I left, pausing often to allow Detective Harrison to write things down in his notebook.

"Now, the wait staff," Detective Williams said. "Do you know who was helping you?"

"I did not catch his name," I said. "But he was a young man with dark hair and a straight nose. Those are the only details I remember specifically. And as I already said, he was the one who felt for Violet's pulse. He tried to help her, but it was too late."

Detective Harrison nodded and wrote everything down, but Detective Williams leaned forward, one gray eyebrow raised. "Did you have any reason to suspect anyone at the restaurant was upset with you? Did Violet send a drink back to the kitchen or offend anyone in any way? It could have been a simple slight. Nothing serious."

I shook my head. "Nothing. Before and after the dinner, everyone at the restaurant was very polite. Wonderful, even. Our waiter continued bringing us drinks throughout the questioning. I'm sure that is noted somewhere."

The detectives looked at one another long enough that I wondered whether they hadn't already made up their mind about what had happened.

"Do you have any leads?" I asked. "I'm sure there isn't much you can share, but I just wonder if there is anything you are able to tell me."

"No leads right now, Miss," Detective Harrison said. "We are keeping our options open."

"In that case, I wonder if you are open to suggestions?"

Detective Harrison nodded, but his older partner stiffened, his top lip pinching into a flat line. "We do not often take suggestions from the public. That is what we are here to do."

"Of course," I said, laughing though I found nothing funny. "It is just that there is a man in my story—Giles Burton—who I believe could be of interest to you. He stopped by our table that night, and Violet seemed nervous around him."

"You noted she seemed uneasy before his arrival," Detective Williams said, pointing to his partner's notes. "It is written here that you noticed she was acting strangely soon after your arrival."

"Yes," I admitted. "But she seemed especially nervous around Mr. Burton."

"Is there a possibility she would have been equally as nervous around any male guest who randomly stopped by your table?" he asked.

"Yes, there is a chance, but—"

"So, is there a chance you are only implicating Mr. Burton because you did not like him? You admitted here that he was 'pompous.'"

"Yes," I said, growing increasingly less patient. "It is possible. Though, I would not say I am implicating him. I am simply pointing out—"

"What?" he asked. "That the young man stopped by your table? You also mentioned Mr. and Mrs. Worthing. Do you think they could be guilty, as well?"

My mother shifted uncomfortably next to me and laid her hand on my knee. It was a warning. The signal she had given me since I was a child. To reign it in. To pull back. To control myself before I allowed my emotions to get the better of me.

I took a deep breath. "Violet did not seem especially nervous around the Worthings, which is why I did not suggest you look into them further. Though, I'm sure, as part of a thorough investigation, you will look into every person who stopped by the table."

Detective Harrison's scowl deepened, the indention in his forehead getting deeper. "Of course."

There were several seconds of silence where Detective Harrison simply scowled at me before Detective Williams exhaled and stood up. "Well, I believe that is everything we came for. Thank you for your time. We will be in touch if we need anything else."

I understood their pairing immediately. The men stood in stark contrast to one another for a reason. Detective Harrison was the young, friendly counterpart to Detective Harrison's gruffness. Alone, they were ineffective. Together, they balanced one another out.

Detective Harrison grudgingly rose to his feet and moved to the door, nodding his head stiffly to the maid when she opened it for him. He stepped outside and began the walk down the stairs while Detective Harrison hung back.

"I am sorry if I angered your partner," I whispered, stepping out on the porch to see him off.

My parents stayed inside in the entryway, and the blonde detective looked back at them to be sure they couldn't overhear us.

"It is quite easy to anger him," he admitted with a smile and a shrug. "He will calm down soon."

"I do hope you will write down my suggestion," I said. "I did not intend to imply you are not doing your jobs, but it is just what I noticed."

"I made note of it," he said, lifting his notebook in the air. "Though, between you and me, Giles Burton is the son of a friend of Williams."

I sighed. "That would explain his hesitation to accept that possibility."

"Perhaps," he said, glancing over his shoulder at his partner, who was now getting into the driver's seat of the car. "Though, rest assured, we will look into every possibility. No one will receive any special treatment."

I smiled and nodded, though I hardly believed him.

"Alice," my mother said from the entryway. "It is raining. Let Detective Harrison find his shelter from the wet and come inside."

I gritted my teeth, frustrated at being spoken to like a child, but I waved to Detective Harrison and, overall, was glad for my experience. If anything, my conversation with the police cemented my resolve to solve the case on my own. I would prove my worth as a detective to myself, Sherborne Sharp, and the police.

7

I spent the rest of the day at home. There wasn't much for me to do until Sherborne Sharp got in touch with me about connecting with Giles Burton. Plus, my mother was more worried than ever after the police left.

"Murdered," she kept saying, accompanied by a shake of her head. "I can't believe it. She was such a nice girl."

"I thought she was the friend of Alice's you didn't like," my father said from behind his paper.

My mother narrowed her eyes at him and then looked to me, worried. "I never said that."

"She was a flirt, wasn't she?" my father asked. "She had a lot of male suitors. You thought she set a bad example."

"James," Mama said, her cheeks going pink. "I would never say such a thing about any of Alice's friends."

I had overheard my mother say those very things before, but there was no point in saying so now. Violet was gone, so regardless of Mama's opinion of her, she was no longer around to be a bad influence for me.

When I left the next morning for Violet's house, however, my mother insisted I take a note for her mother —this one in addition to the letter she had already sent— as well as a small cake made by the cook that morning.

"You could come with me," I suggested. In truth, I did not want my mother's company on this particular outing. I only suggested it because I knew she would decline. Also, I wanted her to remain in the dark about my true purpose for going. If she thought I was being secretive in the slightest, she would become worried.

"No, no," she said, shaking her head. "I'm sure Violet's mother will want to speak with you about...what happened. She won't want to be viewed like an animal in a zoo. It is better for me to just send a letter and stay here. But please deliver our sympathies."

Violet had mentioned at dinner that her mother had insisted I come around some afternoon for tea. I assumed that invitation was the last thing on her mind now, but it was still a small excuse for me to go and visit her.

It had been a long time since I'd seen Violet, and the last time I'd had any real information on her personal life, we had been scarcely fifteen. So, if I wanted to know who she socialized with and how she spent her time, my best option was to go straight to her house.

The Colburn's home occupied a corner lot on a slow, residential street. No one was on the sidewalks save for a tall, dark figure moving ahead of me. He wore a coat that seemed too heavy for the day, and as I got closer to where the man had only a few moments before been standing, I realized he'd been waiting at the gate that led to the

Colburn home. I hoped I wouldn't be the next in a long line of guests who had come to pay their condolences to the family. I wanted to speak with Mrs. Colburn and the staff, but I did not want to be a burden during an already trying time.

A plump maid with curly red hair answered the door soon after I knocked. She saw the cake platter in my hand and reached for it. "The family appreciates your condolences, but they are not taking any visitors right now." She looked past me towards the road. "No matter how long they wait outside the gate."

The last time I'd been to Violet's family home, their maid had been a thin elderly woman named Mrs. Whitlow. She knew me well enough that she would have let me in straight away without question. This woman, however, was new. Or, at least, hadn't been working for the family for more than a few years. Even if she'd heard my name mentioned as one of the people with Violet the night she died, she wouldn't recognize me.

"I actually hoped to speak with Mrs. Colburn," I said, pulling the cake out of her reach. "I wanted to hand deliver this."

The woman pursed her lips. "I'm sorry, Miss, but the family has been receiving a lot of visitors and are not able to see more today. If you will leave me your name, I'll be sure to tell Mrs. Colburn who the cake is from."

"Miss Alice Beckingham," I said loudly.

"Thank you, Miss Beckingham," the maid said, setting the cake on a table next to the door. It was beginning to close when I heard a voice from inside.

"Is that Miss Beckingham?"

The maid paused and looked at me through the crack in the door. "Yes."

"Let her in, Sarah. Please." I recognized the voice as Mrs. Colburn's now.

The maid, Sarah, opened the door, and I saw Violet's mother standing in the entryway. She wore a dark robe over a dark cotton dress, and her graying hair was pinned back at her neck, though strands of it fell loose and wild around her face. Her blue eyes, the same shade as Violet's, were red-rimmed and glassy, ready to shed fresh tears any moment.

"Alice," she choked out, her lower lip trembling.

She had filled out in the years since I'd seen her last, but she still had the same petite build as Violet. Her shoulders were narrow and shaking with oncoming sobs.

"Hello," I said softly, side-stepping the maid, who still looked at me as though I was there to rob the mourning family blind.

Before I could even reach Mrs. Colburn, she sagged forward in a sob, her head hanging low. It had been years since I'd seen the woman, but I wrapped my arms around her shoulders and held her as she wept.

"Thank you," she blubbered through the tears. "Thank you."

"It was nothing. Just a cake," I said. "The cook made it this morning. It is from my mother, actually. She sends her condolences."

"No," Mrs. Colburn said, wiping her nose with the crusted sleeve of her robe. "Thank you for being there with Violet. When...when it happened. Thank you. The police, they told me what happened, and...I'm just glad to know she had a friend there with her. In the end."

This sent her into another sob, and I gently led her back to the sitting room and lowered her onto the couch.

"Of course," I said, rubbing circles across her back. "I'm sorry any of this happened at all, of course, but I'm happy my presence could bring a small measure of comfort."

"The other girls haven't come to visit yet," she said. Then, she looked up at me, gesturing with a limp hand. "I suppose I shouldn't call you 'girls.' You are all women now. Grown and thriving."

"I'm sure they'll come," I said. "They are both shaken. They've never been through anything like this."

Mrs. Colburn turned to me as though she was seeing me for the first time, blinking slowly. "Of course. You've lost someone before. Several people, in fact. Your aunt and uncle, your brother."

A twitch of her brow informed me she was thinking of Edward's crimes. Even if we had wanted to keep them a secret, there would have been no possible way to. Everyone in our circle knew that Edward had murdered a man, but no one held it against us. Though, considering her daughter died in my arms, Mrs. Colburn might take another approach.

I decided it was best to change the topic immediately.

"Nothing ever prepares you to lose a person you love," I said. "But I unfortunately do have more experience with it than most. Dorothy's husband promised he would keep us all informed about the investigation, but I haven't heard from him. Have you?"

"Sarah has been turning away most of our guests," the woman said, gesturing to where the maid still lurked in the entryway. "I am not in the mood to see anyone."

I shifted on the couch. "I can go if you would like. I should have sent word that I was coming over."

"No, no," she said quickly. "I wanted to talk to you. Ask you...what it was like."

My heart skipped uncomfortably. "What do you mean?"

She stared down at her hands folded in her lap, and I saw a tear fall and land on the sleeve of her robe. "Her... last moments. Were they...peaceful?"

I stared at the side of her face, trying to decide what to say. And how to say it.

Surely the police had told her what happened. Mrs. Colburn had to know her daughter was poisoned. Had anyone told her about Violet's collapsing? About the convulsing?

Even before the collapse, Violet had been noticeably on edge and nervous. The evening had not been a pleasant one for her, but no mother wanted to hear that.

I could lie, but would she know? If she knew the details, she would know I was lying to her. Would she see it as a kindness or be angry I hadn't gone with the truth?

"Well," I said, mind flailing, unsure what to say. Finally, I decided on an abridged version of the truth. "It was quick. I don't believe she knew what was happening, and before any of us knew, it was over."

Mrs. Colburn was quiet for a moment and then slowly nodded her head. "That is all I can ask for, I suppose. Under the circumstances."

I sat with her for awhile, listening to her favorite memories of Violet. She was incredibly proud of her daughter. Violet had several older siblings, but they were scattered around the country and wouldn't be in London for another couple of days.

"Where is Mr. Colburn?" I asked during a lull in the conversation.

"Where he has been since we received the news," she said. "In his room. He won't come out for anyone. Not even me."

Her voice hardened as she spoke about her husband, and I could tell I had hit on a sore subject.

"He is taking it hard, but we all are. Our household was very close. Even the maids were fond of Violet. They are devastated. Yet, they still get up and perform their duties."

I nodded, not wanting to interject on what was clearly a family matter. Mrs. Colburn just needed someone to listen to her, and I could do that much.

She sighed. "I suppose I should go and check on my husband again. Perhaps, some of the cake you brought will coax him out. He hasn't eaten anything since we heard the news."

I didn't think it was wise to eat cake after two days of not eating anything, but I didn't say so.

"Don't leave yet," Mrs. Colburn said. "I know you probably did not intend to stay so long, but—"

"I can stay as long as you like," I said gently. "I have no other plans."

She managed a small smile before she turned down the hallway and left me alone in the room.

I looked back to the entryway, and at some point during our conversation, Sarah had decided I was not a threat to the household and left to perform her other duties.

Mrs. Colburn had been such a mess that I hadn't yet had the heart to begin questioning her about Violet's life in the last few years. Though, that was the underlying purpose of my visit here. I needed someone who knew Violet's friends and acquaintances better than I did. Someone who could tell me how she knew Giles Burton and whether she had been acting strangely in the days leading up to her murder.

It would not be so unusual for me to simply ask Mrs. Colburn. The police had no doubt informed her that her daughter had been murdered. Except, Mrs. Colburn seemed reluctant to use the word. Every time she mentioned Violet's death, she stumbled around the phrasing, doing her best to make it sound less violent. It seemed insensitive to ignore her preferences and ask her outright whether she had any clue who could have murdered Violet.

I heard footsteps behind me and spun around so quickly I knocked a pillow off of the couch.

"I'm sorry, Miss Beckingham." A maid, tall with brown hair and an upturned nose was holding a tray of tea. "I didn't mean to startle you."

"I wasn't startled," I said. Then, I laughed softly. "Well, I was. But I am fine."

"I brought tea," she said, stepping forward and setting it on the small table in front of the sofa. "Mrs. Colburn hasn't finished a cup in two days, but I keep making it. It is all I can do."

Now that the girl was closer, I could see the tear tracks across her cheeks and the glistening in her eyes. It seemed that she, like Mrs. Colburn, was constantly on the verge of tears.

Remembering what Violet's mother had said about the servants mourning, I sensed that this young woman might have had a friendlier relationship with Violet than was usual between a servant and a member of her employer's family.

"I'm sorry about what happened to Violet," I said.

She nodded and then looked down at me, her thin brows furrowed. "You were with Miss Violet when…when…"

"Yes," I said, cutting her off before she had to finish the sentence. "I was with her."

Her lips pursed together, and her chin dimpled with the effort it took her not to cry. "She told me she was going out to meet friends, no one I would know. I was surprised because I thought I knew about all of Miss Violet's friends. Turns out, she was right. I do not know you."

"We are old friends," I said. "From childhood. Unfortunately, the dinner was the first time we had seen each other in too long. Now, of course, I regret all the time we spent apart. I should have made more time for her."

"Death has a way of putting things like that in perspective," the maid said, shifting on her feet. "I wish I had said a lot of things to Violet."

I noticed the accidental drop of the "Miss" in front of Violet's name, an indication that I had been correct. Violet *had* been friends with the maid.

"Like what?" I asked. "What do you wish you had said to her?"

I smiled encouragingly, trying to adopt a manner that suggested we were two social equals having a chat, as if there was nothing at all unusual in a guest of the family passing the time in conversation with a household servant. Evidently, this girl had been comfortable with Violet, and I needed to make her comfortable with me if I hoped to get any information.

Luckily, she seemed just as willing to forget the difference in our positions.

She sighed and let her arms swing. "I just wish I'd told her how kind she was to me. How much I respected her opinion."

The maid looked towards the door Mrs. Colburn had disappeared through and then quickly sat down on the very edge of the sofa cushion. She looked slightly exhilarated, and I assumed she was not normally expected to sit down with the company and discuss. I, however, would not turn her away.

Violet's mother had said several of the maids were very fond of Violet, and now this woman was telling me she knew most of Violet's friends. Without entirely meaning to, I had stumbled upon a great resource for my investigation.

"Violet gave wonderful advice," the young woman said. "As her friend, I'm sure you know that."

I did not know that. In fact, Violet had a reputation for being the risk taker. For putting propriety aside and doing whatever she pleased. Virginia always guessed it was because she was the youngest of four. Her older siblings were older than her by a considerable margin, so when Violet was maturing, her parents were not quite as focused on her as they had been on her elder siblings. It allowed for more freedom than a spirit such as Violet's needed.

"I went to her for everything," the maid said, folding

her hands in her lap and shaking her head. "I honestly cannot fathom how I will carry on without her guidance."

"What kind of guidance did she offer you, if I may ask?"

The maid shrugged. "Advice about men, mostly. None of it seems all that important now. Violet pegged me correctly the first time we ever talked. I am a romantic. I fall in love easily, and men take advantage of that. Without Violet, I'd be married three times over already."

The maid could not have been much older than me, so it was surprising to think she had fallen in love so many times when I hadn't fallen in love once. I hadn't even had a serious suitor before.

Perhaps, I should have asked Violet for more advice before it was too late.

"So, even though I was just a housemaid and she had more than enough friends to keep her busy, Violet always made time for me," the woman said. "She always treated me as a friend, and I appreciated her for it. I wish I had told her so."

"I'm sure she knew," I said, reaching out to lay a hand on the woman's shoulder. "I'm sorry, but I did not catch your name."

"Oh, right," she said. "Lily."

I smiled at her and then frowned. "Now, it has been a long time since I spoke candidly with Violet about her personal life, but last I knew, she did not have any serious suitors. I only wonder if anything in her life changed in the last few years that would give her insight to offer you such sound romantic advice?"

"Miss Violet did make her way through the men in

her social circle when she was younger," Lily said, amusement sparkling in her eyes. "She had so many hilarious stories, like the scene that ensued when two of her gentlemen friends showed up at the same party. She spent the evening flitting between the two of them, neither one the wiser."

That sounded more like the Violet I had always known.

"Though, I do not mean to make her sound unladylike," Lily said, clapping a hand over her mouth. "Violet just had a way of telling the story that made it all seem charming. And, after all, she was a young girl at the time. She matured a lot in the later years."

"She did have a special way of telling a tale." I smiled, comforting the girl.

She took a deep breath and continued. "Well, it was some of those very mistakes, actually, that made her so good at giving guidance. Violet had been in most every situation I could imagine, and she knew how to handle them. For instance, she knew when a man I fancied was trying to take advantage of me because she had been taken advantage of many times before."

"By who?" I asked, wondering if this would be where Giles Burton entered the story. Things between them had been tense at the restaurant. I couldn't imagine Violet with a man like Giles, but there was too much awkwardness between them for there to be no relationship at all.

Lily glanced towards the door again and then back to me, her lips twisted nervously to one side. "I'm not sure I should be telling anyone. Violet told me in confidence."

"I would never want you to break her confidence," I said. "But please know I would never tell anyone. Violet was a dear friend. I simply regret she did not have the opportunity to tell me all of these things herself."

Lily nodded in understanding, glanced towards the door once more, and then leaned in, voice low. "You were with Violet in her last moments, and I know she was excited to go to dinner with you. She paced around her room for days after setting the appointment with you ladies. And I could hardly get her to drink a cup of tea before leaving for the restaurant. She could not contain her excitement and sit still long enough."

I wondered whether Lily hadn't mistaken nervous pacing for excitement. Violet wrote the note she'd dropped into my purse prior to leaving. Whoever was frightening her into seeking help from Rose and Achilles had been frightening her for some time. Days, at least. Probably longer.

"Which means," Lily said, studying me for a second, "Violet must have trusted you. Which means I do, as well."

"Thank you," I said. "I appreciate that."

Lily leaned in and began speaking in quick, hushed tones. "Violet had been involved with a man for months before anyone knew about it. She left the house without saying where she was going and would return with flowers or candies or gifts. I knew enough about her to recognize the smile on her face as one that could only be put there by love. Whoever she was secretly seeing, she was smitten with. Well, one night, she came home holding flowers, but instead of smiling, Violet was crying. Heavily. I had to lead her to her room because she could not see through the tears."

"Oh my," I said. Giles Burton did not look like the

heartbreaking type. I would cry if left alone in his company for too long, perhaps, but that was the only reason I could fathom.

Lily nodded knowingly. "Luckily, no one else in the house saw her first. If they had, she was so distraught that she would have shared the entire story at the first bit of questioning. That is what happened when I asked her what was wrong, anyway."

"And what was wrong?" I asked, leaning in, completely engrossed in the story.

Lily raised her eyebrows. "Violet had involved herself with a married man."

I gasped loudly, and the sound broke the spell we were under. Both of us looked towards the doors to be sure we were still alone, and then leaned our heads closer together.

The man could not have been Giles. He did not have a ring on his finger, and he said nothing about having a wife at the restaurant.

"Did she know he was married when she began seeing him?" I asked.

"She did," Lily admitted. "Violet felt guilty about it. She had no intention of hurting this man's wife, but their feelings towards one another were too strong to resist. She explained it like an otherworldly pull. She drew a line straight out from her chest and said it felt as though she was tethered to this man. No matter where he was, she could feel him on the other end."

I grimaced, but Lily looked towards the fireplace, her eyes distant. "It was all very dreamy. I could feel the love washing off of her like heat from a stove."

Yes, Violet had certainly pegged Lily. She was a romantic.

"But the man strung her along for months and then went back to his wife," Lily said, shaking her head. "He told Violet they would be together, and she believed him. It broke her heart, and she was never really the same after that. She stopped going out as much and didn't accept visits from male callers anymore. That man devastated her."

"Who was it?" I asked.

"She never said." Lily shrugged. "Even after he had hurt her, Violet didn't want to risk word of his indiscretion reaching his wife. She still cared for him, even if he chose to be with someone else instead of her."

"How kind of her," I said, barely hiding my disappointment.

"She was unfailingly kind," Lily said. "It is why I trusted her so implicitly. There was a man I thought I wanted to be with. I met him while accompanying the chauffeur to fetch Violet from one of her dinner appointments. The man had a stable job and was very kind to me from the moment we met, but Violet warned me against him."

"What was her reasoning?"

"Violet had seen him be flirtatious with numerous women, though never with the same woman for long. She did not want me to be one of the many, and I did not want that, as well. I broke it off before anything could really get going, and I believe Violet saved me a heartbreak similar to her own. Though, the man took it harder than I expected. He came to the house on several occasions to speak with me. He nearly put my job at risk. Mrs.

Colburn didn't like him showing up here, and the last time, Violet sent him away with a warning that she'd call the police if he returned. It was quite dramatic."

Lily's eyes were sparkling again, and it was clear that in addition to being a romantic, she did not shy away from drama.

"And oh," she said, holding up a hand. "I did not finish my thought. Violet was kind to her married gentleman and kept his secret, but I accidentally found a letter he had written her several weeks after they ended things. He reached out to see how she was doing, and I didn't intend to read it, honestly. I just couldn't help myself."

She looked up at me nervously. "I would never snoop on any of the Colburns. You have to believe me."

"I do," I assured her, patting her hand quickly so she would finish her thought. "What did the letter say?"

"He wanted to meet with her and talk about their situation, but to my knowledge, Violet never met with him. She told me the night she came home crying that she was done with him forever, and I believe she meant it. I put the letter back where I found it and never saw anything about him again."

She stared at me, nodding, and I raised my brows, waiting again for her to continue. Finally, I had to ask. "And was there a name at the bottom of the page?"

Lily leaned back and laughed. "Oh, goodness. Yes. Philip Carlisle."

I ran the name through my mind, but I didn't recognize it. I didn't know anyone by that name. "Who was he?"

Lily shrugged. "I wish I knew. If I ever met the man,

I'd be sure to tell him exactly how much pain he caused her. Violet never told me how she met him or how she came to know him."

At least a name was something. A good place to start.

Suddenly, Lily sat bolt upright. In an instant almost, she was on her feet and across the room. I was surprised, hardly able to track her movement across the room because of the speed, but then Mrs. Colburn walked through the door, and I understood.

"Sorry about that," Mrs. Colburn said, her grief briefly replaced with annoyance. "He opened the door for the cake, but promptly closed it in my face again. I had to find a key to the door. Can you believe that? A key to my own room. It is absurd."

"Don't worry about me," I said. "Your maid brought me a wonderful cup of tea while I waited."

Mrs. Colburn looked over her shoulder and nodded at Lily. "Thank you. That will be all."

When Mrs. Colburn turned to sit down, Lily caught my eye over her shoulder and smiled warmly.

My conversation with her had not gone in the way I expected, but it had been useful nevertheless. She had nothing noteworthy at all to say about Giles Burton, but now I had a second suspect.

Perhaps, Sherborne Sharp would know Philip Carlisle. If not, George could probably help me locate him. Regardless, I would need to learn more about him. If Violet had been involved with a married man, there was no telling the complications that could have stemmed from it.

Perhaps, Philip had grown worried Violet would tell of their affair and killed her to keep her quiet? Or maybe she did tell, and he killed her out of revenge? Or, maybe the wife found out and poisoned Violet out of anger.

Since I had no clue what either Philip Carlisle or his wife looked like, there was no way to know they hadn't been at the restaurant that evening.

Violet had been insistent about taking me with her to the powder room, and maybe that was why. Maybe she wanted to tell me one of her married ex-suitors was in the restaurant.

Not for the last time, I cursed myself for talking with Mrs. Worthing. I was not sure I would have been able to save Violet either way, but the information she could have shared with me in the powder room might have made the difference in the case.

Now, I had no choice but to do all of the work myself. I would do it, however. Whatever it took to get justice for Violet.

8

A fter lunch, a letter arrived addressed to me. One of the maids delivered it to my room.

I closed the door and studied the envelope. Only my name was scrawled across the front in jagged lines with a heavy hand. The strokes were so deep into the paper I wondered how it didn't tear.

When I unfolded it, the writing inside was written with just as much force, but smaller, and the script made it difficult to read. I squinted at the letter and held it up to the window.

Alice,

Unfortunately, I write to inform you that I have been invited to a party hosted by Giles Burton. He is anxious to reconnect with an old Oxford friend and looks forward to seeing me tonight. He instructed me to bring a lady companion. I can only assume you would like that lady to be you.

*I will wait for you around the corner from your house at
seven. If you do not arrive by fifteen after, I will assume you
want your mother to know we are going out together, and I
will knock on the door.*

Giles hosts extravagant parties. Dress accordingly.

Miserably yours,
Sherborne Sharp

WHEN I FINISHED THE LETTER, I caught myself smiling
and quickly bit my lower lip. Nothing about Sherborne's
behavior was amusing. He sent a letter addressed to me
with his name printed plainly inside. More than that, he
gave away where we were headed for the evening.

Had the letter fallen into the wrong hands, it could
have been devastating to my investigation.

Namely, my mother's hands.

Because Sherborne was right. I would meet him
around the corner. My mother did not enjoy his
company in Scotland, and she would not want me associating with him now. If she knew we were going
together, she would do her best to keep me home for the
evening.

WITH ONLY A FEW minutes to seven, I slipped into my
coat, adjusted my lace headband around my curls, and
moved casually down the front stairs.

My father was moving from the sitting room to his study and caught me midway.

"You look very pretty. Are you heading to a party?" he asked.

"I am," I said. "Just a gathering of friends."

He nodded. "That's nice. It'll get your mind off things."

I narrowed my eyes at him slightly. My father was not one to keep track of me or show much concern for anyone's feelings. It wasn't because he was rude, but simply because his focus was elsewhere. Usually on matters bigger than personal troubles. He kept his mind on world affairs and wars and economics. My father dealt better with impersonal matters such as those rather than issues of the heart.

"Yes," I agreed. "It will be good to get out of the house."

He folded his hands behind his back and rocked forward onto his toes. Then, he sighed and straightened his shoulders. "Your mother wishes for me to be more involved in your life. Do you feel such a thing is necessary?"

"I'm fine with the current level of involvement," I said.

"As am I." He moved towards the door and held it open for me, gesturing me through. "Have a good time."

"Thank you." I smiled as I passed, amused at how much my mother would have detested that exchange.

I didn't ask George to drive me, as Sherborne stated in the letter he would pick me up. However, when I turned the corner at the end of our block, there was no car waiting. Only Sherborne leaning against a wrought iron fence, his hands in his pockets.

"Where is your car?"

He stood up as I approached and bent into a deep, exaggerated bow. "M'lady."

"Where is your car?" I repeated.

"What about my flat lent you the impression I own a car?" he asked simply.

He made a good point, but I did not say so. "How are you planning to take me to the party?"

Sherborne sighed and removed his dark gray hat, running a hand through his hair. "You have very little faith in me, Alice. Did I not reach out to Giles and get us invited to a party at his private residence? And yet, you doubt me."

"I have good reason to doubt you," I said. "You know that."

Sherborne shrugged as though he agreed, but did not say so. "Mr. Burton lives nearby. I thought we could walk."

"All right," I said, gesturing for him to lead the way. "We don't want to be late."

"We are already late," he said. "The party started half an hour ago. I do not like being early to things like this."

I decided to keep it to myself that Sherborne seemed like exactly the kind of person who would arrive late to a party on purpose. I followed him three blocks down and two blocks over. The neighborhood was close to the one where I'd grown up, but the houses were much smaller and less ornate. Fences still closed off the gardens and the grass was well-tended, but everything felt more casual. I pulled my coat tighter around my shoulders, shielding my dress.

"You told me to dress in something nice," I said. "Was that just because you wanted me to be overdressed?"

"Do you think only the extraordinarily wealthy know how to throw a party?" Sherborne asked.

"No," I snapped.

He turned towards me slightly, arms held out to either side. "And do I not look like I am dressed nicely?"

His suit was navy blue with thin pin-stripes and his shoes were freshly-polished. He looked sharp and starched.

"You look very fashionable," I said grudgingly.

He walked ahead, a slight kick in his step. "I appreciate your approval."

Suddenly, he pivoted and pulled open a gate to his right that revealed a stone path leading up to a narrow set of stairs and an equally narrow brick home. "Go on inside and find out for yourself whether I tricked you."

I rolled my eyes and hurried up the sidewalk, ignoring the sputter of my heart in my chest. I had to remain calm and relaxed. I was not really here as Sherborne's lady friend or to have a good time. I was here to gather information, and I could not lose sight of that.

At the stairs, I hesitated, waiting for Sherborne to join me. When he did, he glanced over out of the corner of his eye.

"Are you ready?"

I lifted my chin and removed my coat, folding it over my arm. "I'm ready."

When he didn't respond, I looked over to see him studying me for a moment. My cheeks warmed.

The dress was floor length and covered in intricate beading that radiated out from my waist like rays of the sun. The top was a low 'V' with more beading around the collar, and the sleeves were thin flutters of lace that overlapped and tickled the back of my elbow.

Sherborne cleared his throat and stepped forward to knock on the door. "You look nice."

I didn't have a chance to thank him before the door opened.

JUST AS SHERBORNE HAD SAID, the party was elegant.

Even though the house was modest in design, it was filled to the brim with the nicest things—velvet tufted furniture, rich tapestries that stretched from floor to ceiling, and gold-guilded frames on every table. And the guests were no different.

Every woman we passed was adorned in layers of jewelry. Necklaces, bracelets, tiaras, and rings. In fact, rather than feeling overdressed, I worried that I looked simple. When I voiced this concern to Sherborne, however, he placed a hand on my lower back and assured me that was a good thing.

The small house was overflowing with people and we joined in half an hour of idle chit chat before we even spotted Giles Burton holding court in the sitting room.

A group of party guests sat around him in a circle, smiling and nodding as he retold a tale from his college days that, the more I listened, the more I could tell was carefully rehearsed. He had probably told the same story ten times before, perfecting every line.

He paused to leave an opening for the group to laugh, and they obliged. This was when Sherborne cut in.

"You still tell a story better than anyone, Burton," he said, extending his hand to capture Giles' and then clapping the shorter man on the back.

Compared to the tall, dark figure of Sherborne, Giles looked squat. He had a squished appearance, as though someone had overfilled the mold and then forced shut the lid. Certainly not the kind of man I could ever see Violet with.

Giles welcomed the introduction from his old friend, probably only because it contained a compliment, and he introduced Sherborne to the room.

"Another of my Lincoln classmates," he said. "This party seems to be a reunion of sorts. Did you bring a guest, old friend? If not, I know more than a few ladies who would be happy to keep you company."

For a moment, I worried Sherborne would be lured in by the offer of being set up with one of the women here. If only because he would likely be able to swipe a piece of their very expensive jewelry without anyone noticing.

Before my worries could run away with me, however, Sherborne turned and extended his arm to where I stood behind him. I grabbed his hand, letting my fingers slide into the warm embrace of his, and stepped forward.

"I brought Miss Alice Beckingham with me," he said coolly. "She mentioned you two already met."

Giles looked at me, and his expression darkened. "Yes, we did. Under quite unfortunate circumstances, I'm afraid."

"Oh, that's right," Sherborne said. "Violet Colburn."

At her name, Giles looked down at the floor, his head bobbing as though he was reciting a prayer of some kind. When he looked up, he smiled. "Yes, but tonight is a night for lighter things. I hope you both enjoy yourselves thoroughly."

Then, Giles turned to the assembled guests. "I hope everyone enjoys themselves."

Glasses were raised, cheers were shouted, and Giles once again descended into the crowd.

Sherborne leaned in to whisper in my ear. "It seems our host was eager to escape your company."

"You noticed that, as well?" I asked, watching Giles' figure move from conversation to conversation, smiling and embracing his many friends. "Perhaps, you should do more of the talking."

"Perhaps," Sherborne agreed. "Will you be all right if I..." He tipped his head in the direction of Giles.

"Yes, please," I said, waving him away. "I can handle myself just fine."

He raised a doubtful eyebrow at me, and then strolled casually across the room towards the dining room where an array of finger foods and drinks had been arranged. I watched him snag a small piece of bread from the table and wondered whether I shouldn't warn him against having anything to drink, considering the purpose for which we were here.

On second thought, however, I doubted Giles would go so far as to poison an entire party. So, when a tray came around the room, I took a flute of champagne and drank it in one drink, swallowing down my fears. I wouldn't get anything productive done if I was worrying myself sick all night.

Party guests came and went as they pleased. There seemed to be no structure to the evening. Everyone drank and danced and nibbled on food from the table. Most everyone seemed to be acquainted already. Every time I looked to Sherborne, he was in conversation with someone. I seemed to be the only person in the entire house who hadn't found a group to settle in with.

"You look lost," a deep voice said in my ear.

I startled and turned, looking up at the solid frame of a blonde man hovering over me. He smelled sharply of alcohol and swayed where he stood.

"Well, I'm not," I said sharply.

When I tried to move away, he grabbed my arm. I pulled it away quickly.

"Why have we never been introduced?" he asked. "It seems strange we are only just now meeting."

"There are many people in the world I have not met," I said. "I don't find it all that strange that you are one of them."

His brow furrowed in confusion for a moment before it smoothed and he smiled. "I recognize you. There has been a lot of talk about your family in the last few years."

"Thank you for bringing up my family's painful history at a party," I said. "What a wonderful way to engage me in conversation."

Again, the man looked confused, and I wondered whether he could understand me at all. His eyes were glazed over with drink. It wouldn't be long before he succumbed to the alcohol.

"Dance with me," he said.

"I'm here with someone else." I stretched onto my tiptoes and looked around the man, but he stepped into my line of sight again.

"I do not see him."

"Thankfully, his existence does not depend upon

whether or not you physically see him. He is here." The
man had me pinned against the wall, and when I stepped
out to move past him, he blocked my path.

"Dance with me," he said more forcefully this time.

Suddenly, I was a caged animal. My rational mind
faded away, leaving me with nothing but my instincts.
And in that instant, they screamed for me to get away.

Before I could stop myself, I threw back my arm and
cracked my palm against the man's ruddy cheek.

He yelled, not because it hurt, but in surprise. I heard
people around us take notice of the commotion, but I was
still only focused on escaping this tight space with the
very drunk man. While he began discussing my overreac-
tion loudly with everyone nearby, I rushed out of the
room, down a narrow hallway, and into the first doorway
I found on the left.

I slammed the door behind me and leaned against it,
breathing deeply to settle my thrumming heart. When I
was calm enough to look around, I realized I was in some
kind of office.

The room had three walls of bookshelves and a desk
in the center.

It looked too tidy to be used regularly or for
anything more than casual pursuits. I wondered what
job Giles Burton held. Hopefully Sherborne would
gather that information from him. While he did that,
however, I was alone in his private study and it seemed a
shame not to take the opportunity that had presented
itself to me.

I dropped down into his desk chair and began
opening the drawers. Bills and folders full of contracts
filled the drawers on the right and the drawers on the left

were stationery and office supplies. Pens and ink, paper, and envelopes.

Dejected, I pushed away from the desk and scanned the shelves.

Most of the books had something to do with the law in one way or another, which clued me in to the fact that Mr. Burton might be a lawyer of some kind. Though, as I reached the back corner nearest a leather lounge chair, I noticed a series of identical books without any writing on the binding. When I pulled one of the books out, I realized it was a journal.

The dates in the top right corner of the pages told me the books went back several years, so I grabbed the most recent book on the far right and flipped it open, eager to read Giles Burton's personal thoughts.

The first page was from a few weeks before and recounted, in excruciating detail, the proper order of putting on one's clothes according to Mr. Burton. He argued one should start with socks since the feet touch the bare floor otherwise. I did not care enough to argue with him or read further.

After that, a few short entries discussed his comings and goings on a normal weekend and a party he attended, but when I turned the page to keep reading, there was nothing.

Blank pages.

I turned several more pages to be sure, but yes, Giles' diary entries stopped two weeks before Violet's murder.

Frustrated, I tossed the book onto the chair, and it was that toss that revealed the next clue: a folded letter addressed to Giles Burton.

The letter slipped from between the pages of his diary

as I tossed it, and I scrambled to pick it up and unfold it. The script on the front was neat and curled, more feminine than typically masculine, and when I opened the letter, the answer was revealed.

Signed at the bottom, just as it had been on the letter she had slipped into my purse, was Violet Colburn's name.

I gasped and darted back to the top of the letter to read it from start to finish.

Dear Giles,

I received your last letter and the several before it. Sending additional letters will in no way increase the frequency of my writing, so I must ask you to grant me patience. I have been busy of late.

I am sorry to hear your mother has been unwell. Although you insist her spirits would be bolstered by my company, I'm afraid that will be impossible. Send my love and well wishes.

In regards to your request for dinner, I have told you previously and the same remains true now: I am with another man. I have reason to believe the announcement will be made public in the weeks and months ahead, but until then, suffice it to say I am happy and wish the same for you.

Please discontinue your visits to my home and your letters. I am flattered by your persistence, but I will not rekindle the brief romance we once had. It is in the past, and I beg you to come to grips with the present.

Wishing you well,

Violet Colburn

THERE WAS no date on the letter, but based on the deep creases in the folds of the paper, it had been written many months previously.

I did not know enough about Violet's romantic life to know who she had been with, let alone the timeline of her relationships, but I did have to wonder whether the man she was keeping secret from Giles was Philip Carlisle. If it wasn't, why else would their relationship be kept private?

Violet's letter suggested a sense of desperation in regards to the situation with Giles. He was showing up at her home and sending her letters at an abnormal frequency.

Had he threatened her?

When she denied him so clearly, did his affection turn to rage?

It was obvious by the worn state of the letter and its place of prominence tucked inside one of his journals that Giles was affected by the letter in some way and had read it more than once.

Had the letter been his catalyst towards murder?

And had her relationship with Giles been the matter Violet had wanted to contact Rose and Achilles about?

Perhaps, she could not convince him to leave her alone, and she hoped someone else could. Or, maybe she suspected him of going beyond leaving her letters and stopping by her home. Maybe Violet thought Giles was capable of something worse and wanted Rose and Achilles to prove that theory.

I was still deep in thought, staring down at the letter, when I heard voices in the hallway.

"Oh, Sharp, you have not changed in the slightest." Giles Burton laughed.

His voice sounded quite close, and for a second I froze with panic. Then, I jumped into action.

As fast as possible, I shoved the letter inside the journal and then put the leather book back onto the shelf.

I didn't have time to perfectly arrange the books before the door handle turned and Sherborne and Giles stepped into the study.

Giles stopped short when he saw me, eyes narrowed, and Sherborne, obviously not expecting his host to stop so suddenly, ran into his back. Both men jostled for stability for a moment before turning their attention towards me.

"What are you doing in here?" Giles asked, looking around.

"Are you already tired of the party?" Sherborne asked, walking around Giles and reaching out for my hand. I let him squeeze my fingers and bring my hand to his lips, then he turned to Giles. "My Alice does not quite have the disposition for large parties."

Giles pressed his lips into a flat line, unconvinced. "Then, perhaps she ought not to come to parties."

Sherborne laughed as though Giles had told a joke—he hadn't—and it was hilarious—it wasn't. "You'd think we would have learned by now to leave her at home for events like these. Still, I enjoy having her on my arm."

Giles Burton's suspicion seemed to ease slightly when he realized nothing in the room was otherwise disturbed. "I can see why. She makes a lovely companion."

"Thank you very much," I said with a slight bow.

Sherborne placed a hand on the small of my back and lead me towards the door. "May I reschedule that drink for some other time, Burton?" Sherborne asked. "I think I should see Alice home."

"Of course," Giles said. "Any time. I am throwing another get together next week. Come by if you can. It is not as formal as this one so there is no need to bring a lady friend."

"I will check my schedule and see if I can make it," Sherborne said with a grin. "Thank you for the festivities."

He kept his hand on my back the entire way through the party.

As we passed the room with the dance floor, I looked inside and saw the blonde man who had accosted me earlier laying sideways on a chair that looked far too small for his hefty frame. But in an instant, he was gone and Sherborne was helping me slip into my coat and pushing me outside. The moment the door closed, he turned on me, nostrils flared.

"What were you doing in there?" he hissed. "Giles was halfway drunk and ready to drink more alone with me. Can you even imagine the information I could have gotten from him?"

I glared up at him. "You don't seem to care at all about the information I may have discovered."

Sherborne pinched the bridge of his nose and then offered his arm for me to take. He helped me down the stairs and then began walking in the direction of my house. "What did you discover?"

I told him of the journals and the letter tucked inside.

"He keeps a journal?" Sherborne asked, bottom lip puckered.

"Many men keep journals," I argued.

"I know. I do, as well," he said. "Giles simply never struck me as the introspective type."

"Not the point. The point is that Violet was afraid of him."

"She never said that. Unless you left something out of the letter," Sherborne said. "She simply asked him to move on. She mentioned nothing about being afraid of him."

"I could sense it, though."

Sherborne shook his head. "You can't read into things simply because of your own theories. We have to work based on the facts. And the facts are that Giles was, on some level, infatuated with Violet. Every time I mentioned her all evening, he looked on the verge of tears. Whether he poisoned her or not, we don't know, but we do know he is devastated over her death.

"It could be a ruse."

"Giles is not the kind of man who can pull off a ruse," Sherborne said. "Believe me, I've played cards with him."

Aside from the letter, the evening was a failure due to me interrupting Sherborne in the middle of his plan. He dropped me around the block from my home with a small bow as we parted, and then I walked home alone.

As I reached the front door, however, I looked back in the direction I had come and saw a slim, shadowy figure watching me safely to the door.

9

I n the morning, I dressed and went downstairs only to find one extra setting at the table.

My parents were not in the dining room yet, and I did not hear voices indicating we had guests, so the extra plate was a mystery. Until a large figure appeared in the doorway.

"Eating without me?" my sister Catherine asked, laying her hands on her heavily pregnant stomach.

I ran around the table and threw my arms around her. "I wouldn't dream of it. When did you get here?"

She patted my shoulder and then pushed me away. "Late last night, though before you got home. I heard you come in, but I was already in bed with no intention of getting out again. Father said you stepped out with a man?"

"It was more of a business arrangement," I said.

Catherine raised a curious brow, but our parents came downstairs just then, and we all got too busy filling our plates and talking to discuss my possible romantic life.

After breakfast, Catherine wanted to go for a walk. Her doctor had informed her that it was good for the baby for her to get a daily dose of fresh air and stay active. So, I held her hand down the stairs and then took a turn around the back garden with her.

"Edward's birthday was last week," she said suddenly when we were far enough away from the house that no one—not even the cook working near the window in the kitchen—would be able to overhear.

"I know." I sighed. "It was a dark day around here. Mama didn't leave the house all day."

"She hasn't left the house in weeks." Catherine looked at me out of the corner of her eye. "Everyone doesn't need to be so gentle with me. I'm expecting a child, not ill. I can handle the truth."

"It isn't that," I said. "I hardly want to admit the truth to myself."

"Well, Charles thinks that way. When I told him I wanted to come to London for a visit, he nearly cancelled all of his appointments at work and followed me. He is convinced I'll forget how to walk and fall into traffic, I believe."

I laughed. "He cares about you. It is nice."

Catherine rolled her eyes. "For who?"

After their wedding, Catherine and Charles had moved to New York to be near his work, but within a couple of years, they came back to our side of the ocean and settled in Yorkshire. It meant visits from Catherine were much more frequent, though I still didn't get to spend as much time with her as I would like.

"I tried to talk to Mama about what happened when you went to Scotland," Catherine said, directing the conversation back to more serious topics. "She sent me a letter after you both returned home and assured me everything was fine, but I could tell it wasn't. And then I arrived last night to do my best to help and she told me about Violet Colburn."

"Oh, of course," I said, turning towards her, hand over my heart. "I can't believe that wasn't the first thing I said."

"You and me both," Catherine said, eyes narrowed and accusatory. "You were there when it happened?"

I nodded. "Unfortunately, yes. I held her down while she convulsed. It was horrible."

Catherine and I had never been incredibly affectionate with one another. After Edward did what he did and was murdered, our relationship shifted slightly, but more of the change came with age than anything else. As a child, I wanted to be independent and free, which meant spurning my parents and siblings at every chance. Now, as an adult, I understood the importance of having my family and letting them know how much they meant to me.

My sister stopped and pulled me into a hug. For a moment, I let my arms hang, unsure what to do, but then I reciprocated. The exchange lasted only a few seconds, but it felt much longer.

"I can't believe it happened on Edward's birthday," Catherine said, shaking her head. "As if Mama wasn't unreasonably nervous often enough."

"I'm not sure she'll ever leave the house now," I admitted.

Catherine sighed. "She was very distressed by all the

scandal after Edward's death. The official reports maintained his death occurred in a prison brawl, but the newspapers spoke of a possible criminal underground association. Mama spoke to me several times about whether or not I knew anyone called 'The Chess Master.'"

Immediately, the name registered in my memory. At the time of Edward's death, I was too young to be involved in many of the discussions, but I overheard my fair share.

"The Chess Master," I repeated. "Who is that?"

"Mama would hate that I am talking to you about this."

"Need I remind you I am an adult?" I asked sharply. "You can talk to me about whatever you would like."

We were at the back of the garden now, standing under the shade of a tree at the corner of the yard, far from the house or anyone who would care to listen to our conversation. Still, Catherine glanced over her shoulder to be sure we were alone. Then, she leaned in.

"I do not know all of the details, but there was speculation that Edward involved himself with someone calling himself The Chess Master prior to going to prison. I believe Edward was led astray by this individual. Perhaps, The Chess Master even assisted Edward in killing Mr. Matcham."

Catherine was a happily married woman, but pain still crossed her face at mention of the death of her old suitor, Mr. Matcham. He had been her first love, stolen from her by her own brother.

"I always wondered where Edward got access to the poison," I admitted.

"As did I," Catherine said. "The Chess Master might be the answer. And some people believe The Chess Master may have orchestrated Edward's murder in prison."

I gasped. "Do you really believe one man could have that much power? To kill someone when they were already under lock and key?"

"I believe there are many people who have much greater power who we know nothing about," Catherine said ominously, her eyes focused on the hedge in front of us. Then suddenly, she shrugged. "If you want more information, I'd encourage you to write to Rose. She had more of an interest in this topic than I did. Truthfully, I wanted to put it all behind me the moment it happened."

"Does Charles know about Mr. Matcham?" I asked.

"Of course," Catherine snapped. "He is my husband. I would not keep something like that from him. With all of the notoriety our family had in the press there would have been no way to keep that information from reaching him. Even if I'd wanted to."

I could tell by the frustrated pinch of her lips that she had, indeed, wanted to keep it from him. I couldn't blame her.

"I just don't enjoy talking about it," she admitted. "With anyone."

I followed her wishes and dropped the conversation, and several seconds later, Catherine sighed and broke away from the garden path, cutting straight across the grass.

"That is more than enough fresh air for today. My knees can barely stand the weight of this child."

"You still have three more months," I said.

Catherine stopped and looked back at me over her shoulder, eyes narrowed. "Thank you for the reminder, Alice."

I stifled a laugh and followed her inside where the cook had a plate of tea and biscuits waiting for us.

10

Catherine and I spent the entire day indoors with our mother, reading and playing cards and sharing gossip from both London and Yorkshire. The next morning, however, I felt too restless to stay inside.

"I only have one more day in the city," Catherine said. "You really can't postpone your appointment?"

"I'm sorry, I can't. You could come with me?" I offered.

Catherine looked down at her stomach as though that was answer enough and then waved a hand for me to go on.

I smiled, assured her I'd be back in the afternoon, and left.

Truth be told, I did not have any appointment. Not an official one, anyway.

I needed to speak with Sherborne Sharp.

Upon waking that morning, my plan had been to spend as much time with Catherine as possible before she returned to Yorkshire to finish out the rest of her pregnancy and have her child. That had been before I'd read the newspaper, however.

My father, unable to break his bad habit even during a time when both of his daughters were once again in his house, had the newspaper held up in front of his face throughout most of the meal.

I'd become rather adept at ignoring it, but when my mother made her third remark to put it down, I looked over and a headline caught my attention: *Professor Philip Carlisle to be Honored by College.*

I maintained my composure until the end of the meal, but the moment my mother and Catherine made their way to the sitting room, I asked my father for a look at the paper. Surprised by my sudden interest in current events, he gave it to me before pulling a cigar from his pocket to smoke in his study—another one of his habits my mother detested.

The article was short but spoke of a gathering at a local restaurant to honor Professor Philip Carlisle, presumably the same Philip Carlisle Violet Colburn had been involved with, on research he had recently finished as part of his tenure. Everyone in attendance would have the opportunity to speak with the man himself about his important work, and I intended to be present.

SHERBORNE DIDN'T LOOK SURPRISED when he pulled the door open. He was dressed in his finest clothes, his black hair smoothed down to the side as though he'd been expecting me.

"I see you read the paper today?" he asked, one dark eyebrow quirked up.

I had hastily explained to him the other evening about Violet's connection to Philip Carlisle, so he must have immediately understood my interest in the newspaper headline.

"Are you ready to escort me out again?" I smiled up at him, ignoring the flutter of emotion in my stomach at his return smile.

"I had nothing better to do tonight, anyway."

CATHERINE ARGUED BRIEFLY when I left that evening in my finest clothes that it was impolite to flaunt my figure when hers was so woefully out of sorts.

"You are expectant," I reminded her. "You are supposed to look round."

She gasped like I had struck her. "Do not call me round, Alice."

"Honestly, Alice," my mother said, shaking her head.

I apologized profusely and promised her I would bid her farewell when she left in the morning. Then, I walked to the car and directed George around the corner where Sherborne Sharp was waiting for me.

He had on a dark green suit with a slight sheen to it that reminded me of a snake skin. He slid into the backseat of the car with ease.

"What is your plan?" he asked as George navigated the evening traffic.

"I want to talk to Philip Carlisle," I said.

Sherborne turned to me, eyebrows raised. "That is it? Do you have anything more specific prepared?"

Heat flooded my cheeks. "I just hoped to engage him in a conversation."

"About his probably mistress who was recently poisoned?" He shook his head. "That is hardly appropriate party conversation. How exactly did you expect the topic to arise?"

"I don't know," I admitted. "Perhaps, I will tell him I'm a friend of Violet Colburn. I'll say she spoke about him often and seemed to really respect him."

Sherborne shrugged, unconvinced. "Maybe, though that is just as likely to send him running in the other direction as it is to get him talking. Men aren't in a hurry to talk about their mistresses, especially in a professional setting. More than likely, he'll brush you aside for someone else."

Although I tried to tell Sherborne and myself that I had enough skill to avoid that, it soon developed that he was right. Within a half hour of arriving at the party, Professor Carlisle had shaken my hand and then immediately turned tail and ran the moment Violet's name crossed my lips.

Sherborne bit back a laugh.

"I'm sorry," he said when I glared at him.

"You should be," I said. "You are responsible for helping me, and you did nothing. Just stood there uselessly."

"I am your cover," he said. "My task is to keep you company, which I am doing a fine job of."

As proof, he pointed to the drink in my hand which he had recently fetched for me.

"Also, I helped us get in the door," he added.

That was true. When we got to the door, we realized there was a list. The event was open to the public, but attending required pre-registration. Luckily, Sherborne smooth talked his way through the door and brought me with him.

I sighed. "The only good thing is that I finally know what Philip Carlisle looks like."

I could see the man mingling with guests around the room, shaking hands and clapping backs. He looked much more like Violet's type than Giles Burton, though Philip Carlisle was clearly much older.

Wisps of gray hair curled around his ears and at his temples and there were fine lines around his eyes and mouth. He could more easily be mistaken for her father than her gentleman caller.

Still, he was a handsome man with thick brown hair, a strong chin, and a wide smile. It was easy to see how he could charm a young woman into a secret romance.

"I am going to sample the refreshments," Sherborne whispered in my ear. "Try not to get yourself thrown out."

I glared at him as he walked away, but he only smiled over his shoulder and waved. No sooner had he walked away than a woman filled his place. She looked at me and then turned to gaze at Philip Carlisle.

"He is remarkable, isn't he?"

"Oh?" I said surprised. I followed her eyes and realized she was referring to the honoree for the evening. "Yes, very. Wonderful work he is doing."

"Are you a student of his?" the woman asked, turning to face me, her expression suddenly inscrutable.

"No," I said slowly, trying to think of a proper excuse

for being at the party. I could have lied and said I was a student, but I knew the name of a class would never have come to me in time to lie, and even if it had, this woman looked professional. She wore a crisp navy dress with a white collar and sensible shoes. Possibly a professor herself. I had never met a female professor before, but we lived in a modern world now, so why not?

She narrowed her eyes. "Are you here with a student?"

"My date went to Oxford," I offered honestly. "We are just—"

"Here to see Philip?" she asked, thin eyebrow raised.

I nodded. "That seems to be the point of the evening, after all. I saw the event in the paper and wanted to come."

"A young girl like you?" the woman asked, looking unconvinced. "Surely, you have better things to do."

Any hint of warmth that had been in her voice was gone now. This woman didn't want me here, so it was my duty to find out why.

"No, actually. I enjoy meeting the people who will shape our future. It is inspiring."

"I'm sure it is," she said, turning away to stare at Philip again. He was now talking with an elderly man and his wife. He brought the older woman's hand to his lips to kiss her knuckles and the woman beside me snorted.

"Are you a professor?" I asked suddenly.

"No."

She offered no other explanation, and the pinched line of her mouth told me she wouldn't.

"How do you know Philip?" I asked.

Before the question could even fully leave my mouth,

the woman turned to me, her eyes wide and flared with anger.

"How do *you* know him?" she hissed.

I gasped and stumbled backward one step, and the woman seemed to take a breath to compose herself. She straightened the collar of her dress and glanced around to see if anyone had noticed her outburst. Seeing that they hadn't, she took another step towards me.

"You are one of his mistresses, aren't you?" she asked, top lip curled back. She looked down the length of me, assessing me, and then back up. "You look the type. Philip likes them young. Usually blonde, but your brown hair wouldn't be a deterrent for him. Not with a face like that."

I could feel my entire body warming with embarrassment and shock. I shook my head. "I'm not—"

"Not going to speak while I'm speaking," she finished. "I have allowed Philip his fun, but I will not be made a fool of in public. If you wish to come here and stake a claim on him, I would suggest you reconsider. I am his wife and a very respected woman in this society. Even if you were somehow able to convince Philip to leave me, our friends would never accept you. His colleagues would look down on you. You would never fit into our world. Consider, is that something you really want?"

"I don't want anything," I stammered. Then, her words began to sink in. "You are Jane Carlisle?"

She lifted her chin and turned towards where her husband was shaking hands in the corner of the room. "So, he has mentioned me."

"No, no," I said quickly. "I read your name. In the article."

Jane snorted. "Save your lies. I will not allow my marriage to be challenged by you or anyone else. You would do well to leave this party immediately. I saw the way Philip responded to your presence. He couldn't get away from you fast enough. Whatever you said to him, he had no interest. You've tried your best. Now leave."

It was clear there would be no convincing this woman I had no interest in her husband and equally clear that I would not get another chance to speak with Philip Carlisle this evening. Not with his wife watching my every move. So, I lowered my head and began trying to make some sort of dignified exit.

Luckily, Sherborne appeared at my side, offering his arm. He looked straight at Jane and smiled, but spoke to me. "Are you ready to leave, my love? The food at this party is dreadful. You were right, if we wanted a free meal, we'd be better off searching rubbish bins."

Jane raised an eyebrow, and I could see her parsing his words. She looked at me, trying to decide if she'd made a mistake, but I simply lifted my hand in a polite wave and turned to leave.

As soon as we were outside, Sherborne released my arm and made a motion as if to swipe imaginary sweat from his brow. "That was a tense conversation."

"You heard that?" I asked. "How loud was it? Did anyone else hear?"

He shook his head. "Do not worry. I saw the woman approach you and took up position behind her so as to eavesdrop. No one else was paying you any mind. Anyway, what are we going to do now? We can't go back into that party."

"No," I agreed, biting my lip. "Maybe I could wait outside for Philip to—"

"To leave the party with his wife on his arm?" Sherborne asked.

I sighed. "You're right."

"Finally, you recognize my brilliance," he teased.

I smiled and rolled my eyes before an idea struck me, and I reached out and squeezed Sherborne's wrist. "How do you feel about going to dinner somewhere else?"

His eyes went wide. For the first time since meeting him, Sherborne looked panicked.

"At the restaurant where Violet died," I finished.

He eased down, his shoulders relaxing. "Why?"

"When I arrived for dinner the night of her murder, they wrote my name on a ledger at the front desk. Every person who was at the restaurant that night or made a reservation would be written there."

He stared at me blankly, his bottom lip tucked into his mouth, and shook his head. "I don't follow."

"Philip and Jane Carlisle could be on the list," I said. "The police have yet to say when they believe Violet was poisoned, but if it happened at dinner, then the killer would have had to be there. I didn't know what Philip looked like at the time, so it is possible he was there, and I didn't see him. But if he was—"

"His name would be on the ledger," Sherborne said reluctantly. He groaned. "Must I go with you?"

"A woman going to dinner alone is a sad sight, indeed," I said. "Besides, I would draw less attention with you on my arm."

"Are you trying to say I do not draw attention wherever I go?" he asked. "I think that might be an insult to my appearance."

I had no desire to speak to his appearance at all, so I ignored the comment. "Will you come with me?"

Sherborne stared at me for a moment. It was late and growing later. Even though I wanted his help, I would not blackmail him into it. Finally, he adjusted his hat and extended an elbow to me.

"May I escort you to dinner, Miss Beckingham?"

I looped my arm through his and turned away to hide a smile. "You may."

11

Part of me expected the restaurant to look much as it had the night Violet had died.

Patrons standing quiet and shocked on the street outside, onlookers gathering around the edges of the scene to try and find out what happened, police milling around, asking questions and taking statements.

Instead, there were smiling guests. An employee held the door open for us as we arrived, welcoming us inside for a wonderful evening. And the atmosphere inside was warm and lively.

Candles illuminated the centers of the tables and voices and laughter created a happy backdrop to the sight of people smiling and conversing over a delicious meal.

Seeing the utter normalcy of it all made me feel off balance.

"How are you feeling?" Sherborne whispered in my ear. "You look pale."

"I'm fine," I assured him, taking a deep breath to steady myself.

I couldn't allow my emotions to take over. I was here for a job. To gather evidence.

To solve Violet's murder.

"Reservation?" the mustachioed man behind the host stand asked.

Sherborne turned to me for a moment, looking for guidance, before answering. "No, we were hoping there would be a table available."

The host twisted his lips to the side and studied his ledger. *The ledger.*

"We are rather full this evening, unfortunately," he said, not looking at all disappointed to turn us away.

"You don't have a single table?" Sherborne asked sharply.

Without looking down the host shook his head. "No, we do not."

I could read the man at once. He enjoyed the power his position gave him. Even if it was rather limited. Turning people away, directing them to their tables, and seating them where he liked: he enjoyed it. So, he would not take a threat to his position kindly. If we wanted anything from him, it would require flattery. Or pity.

I pouted my lower lip out and hugged Sherborne's arm. "That's all right, my love. You tried. That is what matters."

Sherborne tensed, but I held tightly to his arm, not allowing him to pull away.

"Perhaps, next year," I said, sending a sad smile to the host.

The man nodded once, but I could see the worry beginning to crease his forehead. Before we could turn away, he called us back. "Were you out celebrating something?"

"Our anniversary," I said with a wide grin on my face. I looked up at Sherborne and blinked slowly, batting my eyelashes.

Our attire, originally for Philip Carlisle's ceremony, was a bit fancier than everyone else in the restaurant, though not enough to cause notice. We would simply look as though we were out celebrating a special occasion.

"We are getting married next week, but we have been together for an entire year. And what a year it has been."

Sherborne looked less like a man in love and more like a man headed to the gallows. He turned away, staring towards the front doors, and I shook his arm to draw his attention back to me.

"He is shy about sharing the details of our relationship," I said to the host. "But we'd hoped for a nice evening together. He lost his mother and father in an accident earlier this year and then...just the other day... one of my best friends..."

I pressed the back of my hand to my lips and swallowed back a fake sob. It lured the host in, though. He leaned forward, eyebrows pinched together.

"What is it, Miss? Is everything alright?"

"She's fine," Sherborne said, nudging my arm.

I ignored him. "The other day my best friend passed away. In this very restaurant, in fact."

The man's eyes went wide, and his mouth fell open. "You are...*her* friend?"

I nodded, knowing the man was talking about Violet. "I've always loved eating here, but now my memories are soured from the whole event. I hoped to come and make a new one with my love."

The host was looking around the room as though he would gladly kick another couple out of their table to make room for us. He held up a finger. "Give me a minute, Miss...?"

"Sharp," I said, squeezing Sherborne's arm tightly.

The man nodded and then disappeared into the maze of tables.

As soon as he was gone, Sherborne pulled himself out of my grip. "That was dirty."

"It was the truth," I said. "Well, the second part, at least."

"What if my parents really did die?" he asked.

I narrowed my eyes at him. "Did they?"

"No, but they could have, and it would have been rather insensitive of you to bring it up."

I sighed. "Stand closer to me. I need to use you for cover."

There were other patrons standing behind us, waiting for a table to open up or for the host to take their name, and I didn't want them to see me flipping through the ledger.

Clearly, the host did not see the ledger as important information. He left it sitting on the table top, visible for anyone with an interest to look at. So, it only took a few flips of my finger to turn the pages back to the day I came to the restaurant to have dinner with Violet.

"Hurry," Sherborne said.

"I am," I hissed back.

The host was at the back of the restaurant speaking with a gray-haired man in a blue suit. Neither of them seemed to be looking at me, and even if they were, there was so much distance between us that I doubted they'd be able to tell what exactly I was doing.

Then, a third person approached their group. I was caught by my curiosity for a moment and waited until the man had said whatever it was he needed to and turned away. At that moment, I recognized our waiter from the evening of Violet's murder.

A handsome man, certainly. I was surprised to see him back at work so soon, though I supposed I shouldn't be. Violet's death did not mean he no longer had a need for money. Even if it was difficult for him to return, he could not stop working.

As I watched him move back towards the kitchen, he suddenly looked back over his shoulder, and our eyes met.

We looked at one another for what felt like several seconds, though it couldn't have been more than one, before he turned and continued through the kitchen door.

"Are you finding it?" Sherborne asked, pulling my focus back to the task at hand.

"Make sure no one is looking," I said, running my finger down the long list of names.

Many of the names were crossed out, indicating they had arrived for their meal. Others were scribbled out and written over, leading me to believe the original reservation had been cancelled and been filled with someone else. Finally, towards the middle of the page I saw Violet Colburn's name. The ledger listed her as having three guests.

For a moment, I allowed myself to consider what

might have happened if I'd suggested another restaurant or if we had been one of the parties to cancel and be replaced with another group. Would Violet still be alive?

Those kinds of thoughts were not helpful, though they were hard to avoid.

I took a deep breath and moved on.

Several lines later, I saw Giles Burton's name. The ledger did not indicate whether he had anyone sitting with him at his table or not, and it did not make it clear whether he had called in advance to make a reservation or whether he had walked into the restaurant just as Sherborne and I had this evening, hoping for a seat.

I looked up again to find the host and did not see him. The man in the blue suit was gone, as well.

"Where did he go?"

"What?" Sherborne asked.

"The host," I explained. "Where is he?"

"I don't know. Just hurry."

He said it as though I wasn't already going as fast as I could.

I slid my finger down the list with renewed urgency, skimming over names I did not care about or recognize. Finally, at the end of the page, my hand froze.

Written in tiny letters so as to fit in the small space available at the end of the sheet, was Philip Carlisle's name.

"There he is." My voice was louder than I intended, and a woman standing behind Sherborne leaned around him to see what I was doing. Quickly, I pulled my hand back and let the ledger close to the current day's page.

"You found him?" Sherborne asked.

I nodded, unable to hide my smile. "He was here. In the restaurant. That very night."

"What time?" Sherborne asked with a frown.

I shook my head, trying to understand why he wasn't as thrilled as I was with this discovery. "I don't know. I didn't read it."

"Alice," he groaned. "He might not have made it in for his reservation before the restaurant closed for the night. Didn't you say it closed?"

"Yes." My voice was soft, but the thoughts in my head were very loud, indeed. "We hadn't even received our first course yet."

"Was Philip's name before or after yours?"

I felt like there was a weight pressing down on my shoulders. "After. It was near the bottom of the page."

The woman behind Sherborne was now pushing her way closer to the desk, craning her neck to look for an employee. Clearly, she was tired of waiting on the host and wanted to be seated immediately. With her standing so close, there was no way I could look at the ledger again. So, I tried to recall the paper as best I could.

"There were only a few names after Violet's crossed off on the ledger," I whispered. "Which probably means there were only a few more people seated after we were and before she...died."

"And if Philip Carlisle was at the bottom of the page, then—"

"Then he probably wasn't here yet," I admitted.

"Miss Sharp and—" the host had returned and was looking at Sherborne, hoping for the man to reveal his title to him. Sherborne, however, only leveled his gaze and said nothing. The host cleared his throat and continued. "There is a table ready for you at the back of the restaurant. It is one of our best seats, and we would be honored to offer it to you as an expression of our condolences for what happened the other night."

This time, there was little acting required.

I looked up at the man, my mouth pulled down at the corners, and shook my head. "I'm sorry you went to the trouble, but I'm afraid we've changed our mind. It is too difficult to be here. With the memory of what happened so fresh in my mind."

Sherborne wrapped an arm around my shoulders and pulled me towards the door. "I should get her some fresh air. Sorry for your trouble."

The host lifted a finger and opened his mouth to argue, but before he could say anything, the woman behind us in line stepped forward and expressed interest in the now available best seat in the house.

Sherborne kept his arm around me until we were outside the restaurant and walking away.

"It seems silly to be disappointed that Philip Carlisle isn't a murderer," I said. "Doesn't it?"

"We don't know that he isn't a murderer. We only know his reservation was after Miss Colburn," Sherborne said.

"I know. I just wished that...well," I admitted. "I wished that this could be it. Violet and I were no longer as close as we once were, but she was still a friend of mine. Spending so much time investigating her murder, not knowing who did this to her—well, it makes it difficult to feel as if anything is really over."

"I understand," Sherborne said softly. "You could always stop, you know?"

I snapped my attention to him. "Are you suggesting I should?"

He held up his hands in defense. "I suggested that you *could*. You are under no obligation to investigate this case. If it is difficult for you, then you can stop."

My frustration wanted an outlet, but Sherborne should not be it. He was only pointing out the fact that I was not hired for this case or responsible for solving it. I was neither a private detective nor a police officer. I was simply a citizen and witness to the death. My obligation ended the moment I gave my statement to the police.

Though, it did not feel that way.

I shook my head. "She was my friend. I will do whatever I can to find justice."

Sherborne didn't say anything but just nodded. "Are you ready to go home?"

"Miss Beckingham?" a deep voice behind us said.

I spun around and was met with a tall man in a dark suit with a thick mustache. It took me a moment to place him as Dorothy's husband, the police sergeant.

"Oh yes," I said, turning to him. "What a surprising coincidence to see you again, Sergeant."

"I am glad that it's under better circumstances this time," he said. Then, he shook his head. "Dorothy has hardly left the house the last few days. I've had the doctors over to assure her the emotional distress has done nothing to the baby, but she is still worried."

"Poor thing. I need to visit her. When it is convenient, of course."

"Yes, please," he said. He looked down at the ground and then at Sherborne, suddenly realizing I was not alone. I made introductions between the two men, but it did nothing to extend the conversation.

"Has there been any news on the case?" I asked, pointing back towards the restaurant. "Any new information about how she may have died?"

Reginald shook his head. "I am not working this case, so I haven't been kept up to date. No one has told me of anything new. I am only here because in the chaos of the other night, Dorothy left her purse."

He lifted a small sequined bag in the air that I hadn't noticed before.

"But as Dorothy said, I will be sure to tell you if and when I hear anything."

"Thank you," I said. "I'm sure you are busy enough with things, but if you have the time, I would appreciate it."

The man nodded and then slipped away, taking with him my last hope of discovering anything useful about the case.

I still didn't know enough about Violet's relationship with Giles Burton or Philip Carlisle for that matter. Though, I thought I knew where I could find out more about both.

"Are you ready to go home?" Sherborne asked again.

"I think I have an idea," I said, the idea still forming in my mind.

"That can't be good."

I nodded to myself, certain the idea was a sensible one. "We have to talk with Giles Burton again."

Sherborne groaned. "Alice, it is late."

"Not tonight. Tomorrow."

"We nearly got caught looking through his belongings. There is no way he is going to want to meet with me again. I did my best to play it off, but he suspected something. I could tell."

"He is an idiot," I said bluntly. "Invite him out to lunch, and I'm sure he will come."

Sherborne looked ready to argue, but I squeezed his wrist, shaking his arm lightly. "Please, Sherborne. I need your help. Please."

There was only one person who might know anything about Philip Carlisle, and that was Giles Burton. As a man deeply in love with Violet, he would have known her other suitors. So, I had to speak with him.

Sherborne looked at me, sizing me up, and then shook his head. "You are going to get both of us in a world of trouble someday."

I clapped my hands in success. "Thank you."

12

The restaurant Sherborne selected was a small shop with only a few tables inside—all of which were taken. So, we were forced out onto a terrace. Luckily, I wore a blue sweater over my blouse and stockings with my skirt to stave away the chill of the day, so sitting outdoors wouldn't inconvenience me at all.

He assured me Giles seemed excited about the lunch. The day before—the day Catherine left to return to Yorkshire—Sherborne visited Mr. Burton's home and insisted we all get together for lunch the next day. Having no other plans, Giles had agreed.

"You are sure he is coming?" I asked for the third time.

"As sure as I can be without actually being Giles," Sherborne droned. "Please stop asking."

I opened my mouth to tell him we were behaving far too much like an actual couple when I saw the short, round figure of Giles Burton turn the corner.

His suit jacket fit tightly around his middle, though it

was rather loose around his shoulders, and the legs of his trousers seemed too long for him. I glanced over and saw Sherborne grimacing at the ensemble. He had far less money than Giles Burton, to be sure, yet I knew he would never leave the house in such a costume.

"Mr. Burton," Sherborne said, standing to greet our lunch companion.

I stood, as well, though Giles quickly hurried forward and clasped my hand, insisting I sit down.

"I was glad to receive an invitation from the two of you," Giles said. "You left so suddenly I didn't have a chance to speak to you at length the way I wished."

"I am in total agreement," I said. "That is why I insisted we had to sit down."

Giles turned his attention to me, and suddenly, his smile took on a menacing curl at the ends. His eyes hardened.

Sherborne must have felt the shift as well because he laid his arm over the back of my chair and slid closer to me, his attitude protective.

"I should have guessed it was your idea, Miss Beckingham," Giles said, one eyebrow arched accusingly. "You were, after all, the one conveniently hiding away in my private study during my party."

I was confused by the sudden change in tone, but didn't want to give anything away yet. Not until I knew what Mr. Burton was trying to say.

"I'm sorry," I said, smiling and shaking my head. "I had a run in with a rather inebriated guest of yours, and I made a bit of a scene. If word of it never made it back to you then I will count myself lucky. It was an embarrassing debacle."

"I heard whispers," Giles said simply.

"I naturally ducked into the first room I encountered," I explained. "I hope you did not think I was attempting to invade your privacy."

"For simply walking into my study?" Giles waved his hand dismissively. "Of course not. That would be a leap in logic requiring me to think quite ill of you, indeed. And since you are a friend of old Sherborne's here, I am inclined to think well of you by default."

I smiled. "That is wonderful to hear."

"Now that that is settled," Sherborne said, waving for a waitress to assist us.

"The reason I believe you were attempting to invade my privacy is because you did, in fact, invade my privacy," Giles continued, his voice low and serious.

The waitress approached our table, but Sherborne quickly sent her away and leaned forward. "That is a serious accusation, Burton. I am appalled you would say such a thing. You were always a very sensible man in school."

"Do not feign that we were ever friends," Giles snapped at Sherborne. "Your sudden interest in me seemed surprising, but I am a generous man, willing to make friends in any way I can. As you could tell by the size of my gathering, I count myself blessed to have many friends in my life. I was more than willing to allow you and your guest to be one of them."

Sherborne tightened his arm around my shoulders, drawing himself even closer to me. "You are not behaving in a very friendly way at the moment, Burton."

"That is because you and your woman worked

together to manipulate me and dig through my personal property."

Since the moment I'd met Giles, he had struck me as a slippery kind of man. The type who did and said what was necessary to find his own success. However, I had never viewed him as confrontational. Aside from the small matter of me suspecting him for Violet's murder, of course. So, this turn in his personality was shocking.

"I'm sorry," I said, holding up my hands. "I do not understand what we are talking about. As I said, I only went into that room to escape one of your drunken friends. A friend who publicly assaulted me. Ask your other friends, I'm sure several of them saw what happened."

"Your reason for going into the room may be true," he admitted. "But your reasons for staying were deceptive. Did you or did you not remove a book from my shelves?"

"I did, but I was only curious about—"

"About my private matters," Giles finished. "I can think of no other reason why you would read my personal journal."

"Giles, I didn't—" I started, hoping to somehow turn this disastrous lunch around.

"You did," he said firmly. Then, he sat back and studied me over his slightly crooked nose. "The question is why."

Sherborne sat forward. "You are making something out of nothing, friend. I'm sure Miss Beckingham didn't mean any harm, even if she read your journal."

"I know she did," Giles said, raising his voice so the couple at the next table over turned to look at us. "I keep a letter tucked inside the journal and it was not where I left it. The journal, too, was shoved hastily back on the shelf. I know you read the letter Violet sent me, and I have to wonder whether you weren't at my house in search of evidence."

"Evidence for what?" Sherborne asked. He was playing the mediator while also seeking information at the same time.

Giles glanced around and then leaned forward, lowering his voice once more. "Evidence to prove that I had reason to murder Miss Violet Colburn."

The lack of horror on my face must have given me away because Mr. Burton shook his head. "I knew it. I should have guessed."

"You were there that night," I said. "You stopped by our table and made Violet visibly uncomfortable. I had to know the kind of relationship you had with her. It was my duty as her friend."

He stared at me, his contempt growing by the second, and then placed his hands on the table and drummed his fingertips together. "Well, if it is your duty, then allow me to help you with the chore. I would like to explain fully— as I would have if you had simply asked me yourself—the nature of my relationship with Miss Colburn."

"You know she could not have asked you outright," Sherborne said. "She suspected you of murder."

"And you?" Giles asked, turning his anger towards Sherborne. "Did you think me a murderer?"

Sherborne shrugged. "I have no horse in this race. I'm afraid I'm a victim of blackmailing."

Giles' mouth tilted up in a smile. "Have your vices finally caught up to you, Sharp? I knew it would happen eventually."

Sherborne's cheeks went pink, but he said nothing and Giles turned his attention back to me.

"I liked Violet," Giles said plainly. "For many years, I found her pleasant to look upon and to spend time with. I made this known to Violet on many different occasions in hopes she would return my feelings. For a time, I believe she did. She allowed me to escort her to the theater and to a few shows. I hoped my luck had finally turned. However, that was not to be the case. She began seeing another man."

"Philip Carlisle?" I asked.

"I do not know his name," Giles snapped. "I discovered through a series of acquaintances that the man was married. I tried to convince Violet she deserved better. Because she did. I believed it then, and I believe it now. Violet was the kind of woman who deserved a man who would worship her. I would have done just that."

Mr. Burton's voice began to waver, and he paused to calm himself. When ready, he cleared his throat and continued.

"She chose a married man over me, and that was mostly the end of it."

"Mostly?" I asked.

He looked uncomfortably down at the table. "As you already know from the *private* correspondence Violet sent to me, I tried to convey the depth of my feelings to her several more times after she initially asked me to discontinue all contact. Well, on one such occasion, I went to her house to see if I could catch her leaving for the day and create a chance encounter with her."

Sherborne snorted. "You cannot *create* a chance encounter."

Giles glared at him and continued. "When I arrived, there was a young man standing on the porch. I could not see his face clearly, but I could see Violet's. She was very cross, yelling and gesturing for the man to leave. I nearly stepped in when the man resisted, trying to push his way through the door. However, there was no need. Before I could reach the house, he stormed away and left."

"Who was the man?" I asked, leaning forward, fascinated.

"I did not learn his name," Giles said. "Though, I asked Violet about it later. She was angry that I had been near her home after she had asked me so many times to stay away, but she consoled my jealousy by admitting the man was there to see one of her maids. He was not one of her suitors."

"You are certain it was not Philip Carlisle?" I asked.

"I told you already, I do not know the man."

"Tall, thin, brown and gray hair, especially around his ears."

He shook his head. "This man was young. I only saw him from behind, but he had no gray in his hair."

I frowned at Sherborne. "It seems like too much of a coincidence that she would be arguing with another man."

"Not if you knew Violet," Giles said with a roll of his eyes.

"What do you mean?"

He sighed. "She involved herself in every relationship around her. She could not help but meddle. Violet shared her opinions loudly, and she angered many people in the process."

"Do you mean she angered the man who was on the porch that day?"

"I can't speak to that instance directly," he said. "Though, I know for a fact she had strong opinions about the kind of men her staff should associate with. In Violet's mind, their household staff was an extension of the Colburn family. If she would not be associated with someone, then her help should not be, either. No matter that her help did not have the same connections she did. Violet ruined more than a few relationships due to her own snobbery."

Giles paused and took a deep breath, calming himself. "Though, of course, I adored even her faults."

Sherborne snorted and turned to me. "I think we have more than enough."

I wanted to argue. As long as Giles Burton was willing to sit across the table from me, I was willing to stay and listen. Anything he could say to help me was wonderful. Before I could say as much, however, Giles agreed.

"Yes, I am quite done with this conversation," he said, standing up and buttoning his suit jacket. "I have cleared my name, I hope, and given you enough reason to leave me alone."

"You were at the restaurant that night," I said. "You have not explained yourself on that point. Why were you there if not to see Violet?"

Giles raised a brow in my direction. "I was there for dinner, Miss Beckingham. You were also at the restaurant. Did you kill her?"

"Easy," Sherborne warned, standing up to put himself between me and Giles, though neither of us had made a move as though to attack the other.

"Your lady friend accused me first," Giles said. "I am only making the point that many innocent people were there that night. I frequent that restaurant regularly. It is where I first became acquainted with Violet Colburn. That being the case, she should not have been surprised to see me there."

"Sharp," Giles said, tipping his head to his old school friend. "See to it that you do not contact me further. I have no wish to see you again."

With a final bow and a scowl, Giles Burton excused himself from the table and marched down the street, stamping his heels into the cobblestones.

"Well," Sherborne said, leaning back in his seat. "I think you've done me a favor, Miss Beckingham. I never have to see Giles Burton again."

13

I had not even been home long enough to speak with my mother or father when a letter was delivered to my room.

"This was left for you by a young boy," the maid said. "He said it is urgent."

I closed the door and tore the envelope open at once.

Miss Alice Beckingham,

There has been a fire at the house. The Colburn family is beside themselves. Usually, I would seek Miss Violet for comfort, but she is gone, and I have no one. The family needs a friendly face, and honestly, so do I. Please come when you can.

Lily

I DROPPED the letter on the floor, grabbed my coat, and ran from the house. George drove me to the scene immediately.

Wisps of gray smoke curled into the sky, coming from the back of the house, and people were still lined up and down the streets, discussing the event amongst themselves.

As soon as George parked the car, I ran to the front door, pushing past a man in a dark brown coat with gold buttons along the back.

"Excuse me, sir," I said without looking back.

A few people in the crowd grumbled something about my fighting for a better view, though their complaints stopped when I knocked and Lily opened the door.

Her brown hair was pulled back in a low bun, strands of it falling around her ashen face. She glanced past me at the people watching her from the sidewalk below, and then quickly ushered me inside.

"I'm sorry you had to be a spectacle like that, Miss," she said, voice thick with emotion. "People can be so cruel. Though, I'm sure you and your family know that better than anyone."

"What happened?" I asked, getting straight to the point.

Lily said, "It was horrible, Miss Alice. Horrible. The whole day. I can...I can hardly discuss it at all."

"Try," I urged, curiosity making me impatient. "The fire is out, I assume?"

"Oh yes, hours ago," she said. "But it was terrifying."

"Was it an accident or—?"

"That is what the police want to know," she said.

"They suspect it could have been purposeful. I overheard one of the detectives say it could have been the same person who killed Miss Violet. I personally think—"

Before Lily could say what her personal theory was, Mrs. Colburn rounded the corner with her plump maid, Sarah, at her side.

Ever untrusting, Sarah glared at me and then turned her icy gaze to Lily.

"I was not expecting you again so soon," Mrs. Colburn said. "I suppose you heard of the fire?"

"I did," I said, not explaining that Lily had informed me of it. "I came to see how you were all faring. It has been a distressing week. I can only imagine."

Mrs. Colburn's eyes were red with dark circles underneath, and her lips looked dry. "We are lucky nothing more than the back porch was lost."

"The fire was in the back then?" I asked.

"Yes," she said. "It was started at our back steps. The recent rain kept it from spreading to the garden, but the wind and a servant's penchant for keeping firewood stacked against the house allowed the flames to catch."

"The house is stone," I said, stating the obvious. "So, there was no danger of it coming inside, correct?"

"That is the oddity," Mrs. Colburn said, waving me into the sitting room where I'd sat with her only a few days prior. "The back door had been opened and a small fire caught in the washing room. If it had not been for Lily spotting it and the kitchen staff filling buckets, we may all have very well been buried in rubble."

Mrs. Colburn made no mention of who could have been responsible for the fire, and I did not want to push her clearly fragile disposition any further than necessary.

One thing seemed clear, though. Giles Burton had gone to dinner with myself and Sherborne Sharp to clear his name, and in doing so, had made it impossible that he had started the fire at the Colburn's home. So, if the killer was also responsible for the fire, then Giles Burton was not Violet's killer.

I turned to Lily, who was still hovering in the doorway, and raised my brows in appreciation. She smiled softly. "You are lucky to have such loyal help, Mrs. Colburn."

"I am," she said, smiling up at Sarah.

"Have Violet's siblings arrived yet?" I asked.

"Just this morning," she said. "They moved to a hotel to avoid the chaos brought on by the fire."

"Understandable," I said. "Perhaps, I will pay them a visit at some point, as well. I'm sure you all will be busy."

"With arrangements," Mrs. Colburn finished, eyes cast down toward the floor. "There is a lot to do. Especially since Mr. Colburn still has not left his room. Not even when I told him the fire was threatening the hallway. He stayed put."

"Has he come out at all?" I asked, feeling supremely uncomfortable.

"A few times a day," she said. "To handle a few basic necessities. Otherwise, he hides away and leaves everything to me."

I laid a hand on her wrist. "I'm sorry things are difficult right now."

The woman's tired eyes filled with tears, but she blinked them back. "It is good friends like you who are keeping us all going. Without your kindness, we do not know what we would do."

I could feel her energy flagging, and I needed to find a way to speak with Lily alone. Sarah was keeping guard over Mrs. Colburn to the point that I did not feel comfortable speaking to her directly, especially in her emotional state.

"I do not wish to keep you, Mrs. Colburn," I said. "You should really be resting."

The woman stared straight ahead at the wall for a long moment before she nodded. "Yes, I should. I'm quite tired."

"Allow me to escort you to your room, Mrs. Colburn." Sarah extended a hand and then turned to Lily with narrowed eyes. "Show Miss Beckingham to the door."

I bid Mrs. Colburn goodbye, watching as she slowly ascended the stairs. The moment she was gone, Lily moved to stand next to me.

"The family is in disarray. Miss Violet's siblings only stayed a matter of minutes before they left to find other lodgings. Miss Violet cared so deeply about her parents, but her older siblings are distracted with their children and their spouses. It is a shame." Lily sighed. "You are so kind to visit, though. The house has been so somber, understandably, but it is nice to speak with someone frankly. I'm sure you understand."

"I do." Lily's unearned trust in me felt overwhelming. As though I was a temporary replacement for Violet. It was clear the maid looked up to her employer's daughter a great deal, and now that she was gone, she felt lost. Lily wanted someone to guide her.

She began leading me to the entryway, but I stopped her, stepping close and lowering my voice. "I actually hoped to speak with you about something."

The girl's eyes widened with excitement, and she nodded for me to continue.

"I met Philip Carlisle recently, and—"

She gasped. "Where?"

I explained the event and said I was there with a friend. "The meeting was by chance, but I mentioned Violet's name in passing."

She gasped again, louder this time, and clapped her hands over her mouth. "What did he say?"

"Nothing," I admitted. "He practically ran away from me, but his wife had more than enough to say for the both of them."

"You spoke to his *wife*?"

I nodded. "She thought I was one of his mistresses and nearly had me thrown from the event."

Lily's brow furrowed. "*Mistresses?* That means there was more than one?"

"It seems likely," I said. "Do you think Violet knew that?"

"If she did, she never told me," Lily said. "Though, I do not think Miss Violet would have been with him had she known. She would have ended things even sooner than she did."

"You mean Violet ended things with Philip?" I asked. "Not the other way around?"

Lily nodded. "That is what she told me. Miss Violet was upset about the decision, but she felt it was time to be realistic about where things between them were heading. So, they parted ways."

Violet's letter to Giles Burton said that she believed her relationship with the other man would be revealed in the weeks and months ahead, indicating she believed their romantic relationship was for the long term. So, what had changed? Had she or Philip instigated the parting of ways?

"And when was this development exactly?"

"Months ago," Lily said. "She had been free of him since summer."

I needed some way to verify these claims. Once again, I wished I'd kept in better touch with Violet. Knowing just a few intimate details about her life could have cleared up so many questions.

Lily leaned around me to look up the stairs where Mrs. Colburn and Sarah had disappeared a few minutes before. She was growing anxious.

"Is there any way I could have a moment alone in Violet's room?" I asked quietly.

Lily turned her attention to me, eyes wide and nervous. She bit her lower lip.

"I know it could get you into trouble, and I don't want to put you in a difficult position," I said. "But I would love a moment to say goodbye to her. I'm not sure another opportunity will present itself. Between you and me, I don't think Sarah cares for me."

At that, Lily cracked a smile. "Sarah isn't very fond of anyone beyond Mrs. Colburn."

"Well?" I pressed. "Do you think it would be possible?"

She considered my request, her lips twisting to the side, and then sighed. "Quickly, and we have to go up the servant staircase."

"If I am caught, I'll insist I went wandering," I assured her. "I'll make sure you don't get in trouble."

Lily smiled at me, and I knew I'd just cemented her favorable opinion of me.

When we reached the top of the staircase, Lily moved to take me all the way to Violet's room, but it seemed dangerous with Sarah wandering around.

"Point me to the door, and I'll find it," I said. "I'll also find my own way out of the house. That way you can busy yourself with another task."

Lily pointed me to the third door on the right and then made me swear I would visit her again.

"I know we come from different worlds, Miss Beckingham, but I can't help but feel that any friend of Violet's is a friend of mine," she said.

"I'll visit," I promised. I meant it, too. For some unexplainable reason, I quite liked Lily.

I tiptoed silently down the hallway to Violet's room and slipped inside before Sarah could catch me in the act. Just before I closed the door, I turned to wave to Lily one final time, but she had already gone back downstairs.

Violet's room smelled strongly of flowers and when I turned on the light, I realized it was because of the numerous bouquets spread around the room. All of the floral arrangements were white and the small cards of sympathy affixed to the vases told me they were funerary bouquets. No doubt gifts sent from mourners.

There was no telling when another arrangement would arrive and be brought to Violet's room, so I had to make my work quick.

I scanned the room, searching for the most likely place where Violet would keep a journal or store her letters.

Much as I expected, the room was a mess. Clothes

were draped over the chair in front of her wardrobe and over the trunk at the end of her bed. Shoes lay where Violet had likely kicked them off, and open containers of makeup covered her writing desk.

There were no bookshelves like in Giles Burton's study and her writing desk did not have a drawer like mine did to allow for the storing of sensitive letters. Anyway, if I understood the relationship between Lily and Violet well enough, then it was likely Lily was in her room regularly. Violet would not keep anything personal —especially in relation to her married suitor—where it could be seen by Lily or any other members of the household. She would have hidden it.

I knelt down next to her bed and peeked underneath, but aside from dust, there was nothing.

Then, I searched through the drawers of her dresser, pulling each drawer out slowly so as not to draw the attention of anyone else upstairs. I rifled through Violet's delicates and underclothes, but there was nothing hidden away in the likely places.

I was moments away from giving up the search altogether, too nervous about being found out by Sarah to keep up what could be a fruitless search, when I took a step back from the dresser and felt the floor shift strangely beneath me.

When I lifted my foot, there was a soft thud, and I realized it was the wooden floorboard falling back into place.

I once again pressed my heel into the wood and the board lifted, exposing a secret hiding place underneath the floorboards.

I dropped down to my knees and pulled the board free as quietly as possible. Then, I reached inside.

Immediately, I found a thick bundle of something. When I pulled it free of the floorboard, I realized they were bound together letters, each one addressed to a *Miss Violet Colburn* from a *Prof. P. C.*

Professor Carlisle's code name was not nearly covert enough to make him unrecognizable.

I untied the silk ribbon around the bundle and sorted through a year's worth of letters from the man Violet had kept secret from her family.

As much as I wanted to read them all, I didn't have time. So, I skimmed a few letters in the stack, trying to ignore the feeling that settled in my stomach while reading Philip's professions of love to a woman who was not his wife.

Reading them, I could see why Violet would fall for such a man. *My pearl,* he called her. *My love, my light, my forever flower.* Philip was either deeply in love with Violet or he was a skilled actor. Otherwise, I could not understand how he could write such things to Violet and several other women he was seeing in addition to his wife.

The letters revealed little about the romantic relationship. So, I set the bundle aside and reached into the floor again. This time, I found a book. Simple, clothbound, with a metal clasp on the right hand side.

It looked like a diary and upon opening it, I discovered that it was.

Violet dated every entry and signed her name at the bottom with a small flower scribbled next to the 't.' I flipped towards the last few entries, hoping to see something about her being finished with Philip Carlisle. Something that would explain why their association ended.

Instead, I found a large gap of three months where Violet wrote down nothing in her journal. She did not discuss the day's events or her feelings. She recorded nothing for three months until she opened her journal one week before her death.

I wrote to Philip for the first time in months. It is an important matter, one involving my safety, but he has not responded. Surely, he thinks I am lying to get his attention, but I am not. I know he only needs time to see things the way I do. While he decides how to move forward, I will wait for him. That is what he asked me to do, isn't it? To wait for him? To love only him?

He thinks I do not know of the other women he sees, but I am not a fool. However, I know he loves me most. That is why he is so tormented. He feels he is being dishonest with his wife, so he has to discontinue seeing me. I know with certainty he is still seeing the other women, but they are simply a way to fill time. A way to keep his brilliant mind occupied. I am the one who causes him distress, which means I am the one he loves.

It feels good to be loved by him, though loving him hurts me deeply. I suppose I can understand Giles' pain on some level. He loves me, too. Though I feel nothing for him. There must be deep pain in that arrangement. To care deeply for someone who does not want you. I hope he will be cured of

his feelings soon enough. I have made myself plain and can
do no more.

THE ENTRY RETURNED to the subject of Philip Carlisle, but I was running out of time and skimmed the rest. One thing that came through clearly was that likely until the very day of her death, Violet was waiting for Philip Carlisle to return to her.

And now he never would.

Like Giles had persisted with his affections for Violet, had Violet done the same to Philip? Had she shown up at his home over and over again until he believed he had no choice but to end her life?

Then there was Jane Carlisle, who had boldly confronted me at her husband's ceremony. Had she finally reached the end of her rope where Violet was concerned? Had she poisoned the young woman?

In the letter, Violet alluded to the idea that she was in danger and had reached out to Philip, yet he had not answered. Was it possible Philip himself had been the threat and Violet had been unaware?

A noise in the hallway tore me from my thoughts, and I quickly hid everything away in the floor and replaced the wooden plank. If necessary, I would return for this evidence. Until that became necessary, however, I would allow Violet's secrets to remain her own.

Listening carefully at the door, I slipped from the room, descended down the servant's stairwell, and left through the front door without anyone seeing me leave.

14

The next day, a letter arrived at my door again. This time, the maid did not seem keen to elaborate on who had given it to her or for what purpose. She simply handed it to me and left.

The usual spot will do.

I recognized Sherborne's handwriting.

I dressed in a rose-colored cotton gown with brown two-toned oxfords and a white sweater. My hat was pulled down low over my ears to shield me from the autumn winds that had begun to pick up.

Leaves fell from the trees, papering the sidewalks in color, and the skies seemed even more full and gray than usual. Winter would not be far away now.

Sherborne Sharp looked like a rain cloud incarnate waiting for me just around the corner from my house.

He wore a gray suit with shiny black shoes and a matching hat.

"What a surprise," I said. He still had not seen me and turned around, eyebrows lifted at the sound of my voice.

"I do love surprising people," he mused with no real hint of amusement. "I had not heard from you in an entire day and thought it would be wise to check on you."

"I am not a child," I said rather crossly. "Besides, our arrangement is that you be available to me when I need you. You are under no obligation to reach out unless I first contact you."

"You say 'arrangement' as though I had a choice in the matter."

"You did, did you not?" I asked. "Your choice was to help me or be exposed to all of your peers. Though, if Giles' comment at the end of our meeting yesterday meant anything, many people in your life already suspect you of untoward behavior."

He dismissed my comment with a wave. "Giles Burton said so many dull things yesterday I could scarcely keep up."

"I was rather interested," I admitted.

Sherborne shrugged. "Have you discovered anything new since yesterday?"

Quickly, I relayed the letter Lily sent to me and my visit to Violet Colburn's home. I told Sherborne of the letters and the diary entry. Of Violet's obsession with the married man, even up until her death.

"The maid sent for you herself?" Sherborne asked, forehead wrinkled in confusion. "You'd only met the woman once before?"

"Yes, but she was very close with Violet and is going through a difficult time. She was in search of a friend."

"She should have a friend of her own station," he said. "She should not be reaching out to Violet's friends.

If Mrs. Colburn knew, I'm sure the girl's position would be in danger."

"We were careful," I said. "Besides, I am grateful for the information. It helped me a great deal. Without her invitation, I never would have thought to speak with the Carlisles again."

Sherborne paused, blinking slowly. "Excuse me?"

"I know my first conversation with Philip, and with Jane, for that matter, did not go to plan, but I must speak with them again. Violet believed Philip was coming back for her. What did that belief lead her to do?" I shook my head with the possibilities. "If Violet had approached him when his wife was nearby as I had or if she insisted on seeing Philip after he had asked her to stop, then—"

"They could kill," Sherborne finished.

"Exactly," I said, excited he understood where I was headed.

"No, Alice," Sherborne said, stepping closer to me, his head lowered. "They could kill you. Do you not under-stand the danger you are putting yourself in?"

I sighed. "You and others said the same thing at Druiminn Castle, but I solved that mystery."

"And nearly got killed in the process," he said. "Now, you are dealing with someone who killed Violet Colburn in a room full of people. Someone who may have set fire to the Colburn's home. And why? Now that Violet is dead, the fire was simple cruelty toward her family. The person you are searching for is not a rational person. They will not surrender when you've solved the crime. They will kill you to conceal their secrets."

Sherborne was standing over me, his shape blocking out what little light managed to creep from beneath the crowds, and for the first time, I realized how foolish I'd been.

"Let the police handle this," he continued. "I passed by the restaurant on my way here and it was closed for investigation. The police are looking into the matter, and I'm sure they will come to a conclusion. They may not know Violet's life as intimately as you do now, but they are at the scene of the crime. They can see things that we cannot, no matter how many people we talk to or journals we read through. Allow them to do their job and keep yourself safe."

I had held Sherborne's secret over his head. Had threatened to expose him and ruin his reputation if he did not help me. It occurred to me now to wonder what had stopped him from killing me to keep me quiet, just like Violet's killer might. I had made several mistakes during the course of my investigation, but the biggest one might just have been trusting Sherborne Sharp.

"Alice?" he asked, eyes turning down at the corners in concern. "Are you listening to me?"

"Are you threatening me?" I asked, putting a few more steps of distance between us. "Is this because I blackmailed you?"

His forehead wrinkled, and he shook his head. "Of course I'm not threatening you. I'm trying to help you understand the danger you are putting yourself in."

"And for the first time, I do," I said. "Thank you. Clearly, you are not as carefree as you want the world to believe."

Sherborne sighed. "You are a maddening woman, Alice Beckingham. I try to save your life, and you charge me with attempting to threaten it. Do you not see how silly that is?"

I didn't know anything anymore.

He threw his hands up in the air. "That is it. I am done with this. You caught me attempting to steal something from your mother, and I believe I have more than paid for that crime. From this moment on, my debt to you is paid. I will not respond to any more threats of blackmail on that charge."

We stared at one another for a few seconds, a wordless challenge passing between us, and then Sherborne turned on his heel and marched down the street without looking back.

~

THE MOMENT I WAS ALONE, the fear I'd felt in Sherborne's presence eased and my head cleared.

I felt foolish.

Yes, Sherborne could have hurt me, but he hadn't. He had never even attempted to, so why had I mistrusted him?

Part of it, I knew, was because he spoke to me as though I was a child, incapable of handling myself in my own investigation.

The majority of it, though, came from my own disappointment.

Disappointment in the fact that the man I thought was my partner, actually had little faith in me. Even though our relationship had begun under the pretense of blackmail, I thought Sherborne found a small amount of enjoyment in working with me. I thought he trusted my opinion.

Now, however, I knew that he would rather I step aside and allow the police to investigate. *For my own protection.*

I sighed and walked around the block, not yet ready to return home.

Cousin Rose had always made her investigations look easy. Of course, I hadn't been around for most of them, but still, it felt like I should be getting better at this by now. It seemed like I shouldn't be getting caught by the likes of Giles Burton or frightened away by a scorned wife.

I should have more clues, more evidence, more of an idea where my investigation was heading.

A heavy mist hung in the air, and I paused on the corner, watching people slip out of their homes, umbrellas opened above their heads. One woman draped a jacket over her baby's stroller as she hurried down the street. Another man held a paper above his head.

I could feel the moisture clinging to my skin and curling the ends of my hair, but my thoughts were elsewhere.

Giles had been my prime suspect from the start, yet, I could no longer bring myself to think of him as guilty of the crime. While I detested the man's character, he seemed honest in telling us of his relationship with Violet, and according to what Violet had written in her journal, his story was verified. Giles' only crime was loving a woman who would never love him back.

The Carlisles, while the next suspects on my list, were tied only loosely to the crime in that Philip Carlisle once had a relationship with Violet. Their relationship was illicit, though not criminal, so I had nothing to connect him to the poisoning aside from having a reservation at the restaurant the night of the murder.

Talking with them again would not be possible with Jane Carlisle keeping such a careful watch on her husband's activities, especially where it concerned female acquaintances. So, I would have to find information about them and their whereabouts from some other source.

I sighed and turned to begin the walk home when the idea seemed to strike me all at once.

The restaurant.

Sherborne had mentioned that the restaurant was closed for a police investigation and that was precisely where I needed to go next.

I had theories and letters and possible motives, but I didn't have the one thing that could propel me towards a solution: the scene of the crime.

My memories of the restaurant were muddled with images of Violet collapsing to the ground, convulsing in my arms. Even when Sherborne and I had returned, I'd been so focused on the ledger that I hadn't looked around.

How many people actually had access to Violet's food and drink? How close were the neighboring tables? Were there any blind spots in the restaurant that would allow someone to tamper with our orders without us seeing?

I didn't know whether I would be able to answer any of these questions by simply returning to the restaurant, but it couldn't hurt. My investigation had stalled out, especially now that Sherborne was no longer willing to help me. I needed something to get my investigation on track, and returning to the restaurant seemed like the best option.

So, rather than taking a right and returning home, I went left and began the long walk back to the scene of the crime.

15

A chain was wrapped around the front door of the restaurant and a sign in the window announced to the public that it was closed for an investigation. I was certain the owners of the establishment did not appreciate that form of publicity. When I had been there with Sherborne previously it had seemed that they had been intent on remaining open but the police must have prevailed, forcing them to lock the place up.

There was no sense trying the front door because of the chains. Unless I wanted to shatter the window, I needed to find another way in.

Large drapes hung over the windows, but as I walked slowly past the front of the restaurant, I was able to peek through a crack in the curtain and see that there were no lights on inside. The restaurant may have been closed for the investigation, but there was no one currently inside investigating.

Which worked out perfectly for me.

I continued around the block and then cut through the alley that ran behind the restaurant. My shoes stuck to the damp ground and the air was thick with the sickly-sweet smell of rotting garbage.

I counted the buildings as I passed to be sure I would stop at the correct door. When I reached the restaurant, however, I realized that was not necessary. Just as there had been a sign alerting everyone to the closure on the front window, there was a similar sign affixed to the rear door.

Unlike around front, there were no chains on the metal door at the rear of the building. I cautiously stepped forward and reached for the handle, but as I did, I realized not only were there no chains, but the door was not even closed. It had been propped open a few finger widths, and when I looked down the length of the frame, I saw a wooden kitchen spoon wedged against the frame to hold the door open.

I imagined an officer had propped the door open to step outside and had forgotten he'd done it, which was perfect luck for me. I pulled the door open slowly, slipped inside, and then closed it, making sure to keep the spoon there in case the door locked behind me.

The first room I entered was a store room. In the dimness, I could make out the shelves and the food stacked on them. Rice and beans and canned goods were stacked to the ceiling along with large tubs of sauces and endless bottles of liquor. A single door ahead with a window in the center provided the only light, though it was still meager.

I moved towards it and opened the door into the kitchen.

The room was still and quiet, unnaturally so for what was likely a very busy kitchen most of the time. The counters were scrubbed clean, meaning the police had given the staff an opportunity to close down the kitchen properly.

How much evidence had been lost in that process?

The police believed it could have been someone at the restaurant who had committed the crime, though I wasn't certain.

Especially since the Colburn's home had been set on fire. The person who killed Violet clearly had a personal connection to the family, and surely Violet would have mentioned if she had known someone who worked there. In fact, knowing Violet, she probably would have refused to go to the restaurant and be seen conversing with anyone in a service profession.

So, what was I doing there?

I walked around the kitchen, running my finger along the edge of the countertops, looking for something I wasn't sure I'd recognize even if I saw it.

There was an obvious preparation area for the food and then a long counter just in front of the doors where finished plates would be set to be carried away by the servers. I had seen our own waiter go in and out of the swinging doors all evening, carrying plates and drinks.

With a full kitchen staff, it would be difficult to tamper with any of the food in the kitchen. The room was wide open and, with the lights on, bright. Not the place to prepare a poison.

I walked around the table and pushed open a swinging door with a circular window in the center.

The chairs in the dining room were sitting on top of

the tables and the white tablecloths had been stripped, leaving the wooden tables bare. I could see them sticking above a half-partition in the corner where the waiters and waitresses kept additional napkins, glasses, and silverware.

Empty of people and disassembled as it was, the room looked far less romantic than usual. The soft glow of candlelight was not there to lend the room an ambience or reflect in the mirrored panels along the walls that ran from floor to ceiling.

The space looked empty and cold and gray.

Clearly, there was nothing here.

No obvious evidence sitting on the floor, dropped by the culprit the night of Violet's death and left for days afterward.

I felt foolish for thinking I'd be able to walk into the room and see something the police hadn't found in their days of investigating. I felt foolish for thinking I could solve this crime at all.

Perhaps, solving the murder at Druiminn Castle had been a lucky guess, a series of events outside of my control. Maybe it had nothing to do with my abilities in the slightest.

Maybe I should have called Rose and Achilles the way Violet had wanted to in the first place.

I moved slowly towards the front of the restaurant, growing more and more defeated with every step. I should have gone home. I should have listened to Sherborne and the voice inside my head that questioned my abilities. I should not have taken on this task.

Perhaps, I was too close to the crime.

Violet had been my friend. I wanted to give her

justice, but now that I had failed, I felt responsible. Responsible for her death, for not seeing the signs of her discomfort earlier. Maybe if a doctor had been called sooner, she could have survived. Maybe if I'd gone into the powder room with her rather than speaking with Mrs. Worthing I would have noticed something important, something lifesaving.

Tears burned the backs of my eyes. Angry and embarrassed, I tried to hold them back, but they leaked down my cheeks and over my lips.

They flowed heavily enough that I couldn't see. So, I pulled a chair down from the nearest table and sat down, shoulders shaking.

I didn't know how long I sat there drowning in pity, but when I looked up, the light from outside seemed to be slicing through the room at a slightly different angle. And either my eyes had simply adjusted to the gloom or it was brighter.

My parents didn't know I had left the house. No one knew where I was. I was an adult, but my mother still expected to know where I was going. I needed to get home.

Drying my eyes, I sat tall and took a deep breath.

I would let the police handle this. Just as Sherborne had suggested.

The next time I saw him, if he ever wished to see me again, I would apologize. Charging him with ill-intentions, threatening me, no less, had been wrong. He had done nothing but assist me in my wild hunt for the murderer even though I was blackmailing him. Sherborne Sharp had proven himself a better person than me, and he deserved an apology.

I laid my palms flat on the table, preparing to stand, when I looked around the room and realized I was at the exact same table I'd been in the night of Violet's death.

The same seat, even

The room looked different with the chairs on top of the tables and with no people, but I had the same view of the kitchen and the preparation area in the corner. I could look over my shoulder and see the host stand where the man with the mustache had stood. I could see the door where patrons had rushed out when the police arrived to take Violet's body.

The room seemed to come alive around me.

The ghostly sound of silverware clinking together filled the air. The imagined sound of laughter and conversation. Swirls in the shadows around the room took the shapes of waiters whisking food and drinks and fresh napkins to tables.

I could see Violet next to me.

Her rich brown hair and large blue eyes.

With the knowledge I'd come to possess since her passing, I could see the turmoil in her expression now. The fear and longing.

I remembered Violet glancing around the room as though looking for someone. As Virginia and Dorothy talked about their lives, about Dorothy's husband and unborn child, about Virginia's education, Violet kept looking to the door as though expecting someone.

Philip Carlisle.

The idea came to me all at once.

His name had been on the ledger. He had a reservation at the restaurant for that very night. Violet must have known.

Just a week before her death she had written of her love for him. She had expressed her desire to be with him, and her belief that he desired to be with her, as well.

Violet had selected that restaurant not because she liked it, but because she could not stay away. From Philip or his wife. Even just a glimpse of him was enough of a reason for her to go out with friends she had not spoken with in years.

So, Philip's name on the list did not mean he had anything to do with her death, but it also was not a coincidence. Violet was following the man.

I looked back to the chair where Violet had been sitting, and I could see her sitting there as though we had never left the restaurant. As though she had never been poisoned. I wanted to reach out and shake her, rattle the information from her.

"Who were you afraid of?" I whispered quietly to myself.

Giles Burton came to that restaurant often, and though he had been in love with Violet, the fire at the Colburn house potentially ruled him out. He had been at lunch with me at the time, so unless he had an accomplice, he could not be the murderer.

Besides, I'd watched Giles carefully from the moment he approached our table. Violet had been unnerved by him, and I'd noticed. If he had slipped anything in her drink, I would have seen. At least, I liked to think so.

Suddenly, I turned to look towards the corner of the room.

The preparation area in the corner was covered partially by a partition wall.

Waiters and waitresses moved back there all evening. Our own server had fetched our refills from there.

Could it have been tampered with there? By someone at the restaurant?

But why?

Violet had a list of people who might have been upset with her, but none of them had any connection with the restaurant aside from eating there occasionally.

Suddenly, I remembered something Lily had said. *There was a man I thought I wanted to be with. I met him while accompanying the driver to fetch Violet from one of her dinner appointments.*

Lily had spoken to me of a man she once liked who Violet warned her against. Giles Burton, too, had said plainly that Violet often meddled in the personal lives of her help. *I know for a fact she had strong opinions about the kind of men her staff should associate with. In Violet's mind, their household staff was an extension of the Colburn family. If she would not be associated with someone, then her help should not be, either.*

Lily said the man had come to the house several times to speak with her but had ultimately been turned away by Violet, and Giles confirmed this story when he went to the house in hopes of seeing Violet and found her talking with a man on the porch. According to him, the conversation had been tense.

So, the man was, in Violet's eyes, unsuitable for Violet because of his station in life and his flirtatious ways, he worked in a place that would put him at the location of one of Violet's dinner meetings, and he knew where the Colburns lived. The man Lily had refused on Violet's advice had argued with Violet to the point she had threatened to report him to the police should he ever return.

Could that man have worked at the restaurant? Could he have tampered with Violet's drink?

My heart jumped in my chest. The disappointment I'd been feeling only a moment before was replaced by new purpose.

I'd dismissed Lily's story of her almost suitor as nothing more than a sign of her devotion to Violet, but now I needed to speak with her about it desperately. I needed to know the man's name. If he worked at the restaurant, the police needed to know immediately.

I stood up and was about to replace the chair on top of the table when I heard a faint thud come from the back of the restaurant.

I froze, my breath catching in my throat, and stared back at the kitchen door.

Through the small window, I could see a flutter of movement on the other side.

Someone was here.

Maybe the police or an employee. Perhaps, the owners.

Either way, no one would take kindly to me sneaking onto the scene of the crime. I could explain to the officers that I simply wanted to come and honor the memory of my friend, but that wouldn't stop them charging me with trespassing or maybe something even worse.

The front doors were chained, and again, unless I wanted to shatter the glass—an act that would cause more trouble and injury than it was worth—the only way out of the restaurant was through the back door. The door which was now guarded by the stranger moving around in the kitchen.

I crouched down and hoped the person was simply there to grab something they'd left in the kitchen and would leave without returning to the dining room, however, that dream died when the kitchen door swung open.

The person hadn't seen me yet because they'd opened the swinging door by walking backwards through it, giving me a view of their long dark coat. With gold buttons.

As the stranger spun around, a memory flickered to life in my mind, growing more certain like a match catching a log and flaring into a roaring fire.

I'd seen that coat before. Those buttons.

Twice now. Outside the Colburn's home.

Whoever was walking through the door had been at Violet's house before, including the day of the fire.

Whoever was walking through the door had a connection to Violet's home and the scene of her death, which could not be a coincidence.

Whoever was walking through the door was the killer.

I held my breath as the figure turned, walking confidently into the dining room, clearly believing they were alone. But even crouched down as I was, it took the man only a second to recognize he was, in fact, not alone. As soon as his eyes landed on me, he froze. His mouth fell open, his eyes went wide, and he froze mid-step.

Then, he tilted his head to the side and smiled. A smile I recognized. A smile that, the night of Violet's death had been friendly and accommodating, but now seemed menacing.

"What are you doing here, Miss?" he asked.

I had a similar question for him, though I knew what his answer would be. *I work here, Miss. Don't you remember? I was your waiter the night your friend died.*

Our waiter he certainly was. Though, I now knew without a shadow of a doubt that he was Violet's killer, as well.

16

*O*ur waiter has a fine face, I'd said.

I'm certain he does not have the personality to match, Violet responded. Later adding, *I wouldn't allow that man to take out my help.*

At the time, I'd thought she was being a snob. I'd thought her admission that she would bar the waiter from associating with her help was hypothetical. Now I could see that it had been based in fact.

Our waiter had expressed interest in her housemaid, and Violet had seen to it that the relationship ended. Our waiter, the man whose name I never bothered to learn and whose *fine face* I had not remembered enough to recognize him in the crowd outside the Colburn's home the day of the fire, had persuaded Lily to see him. He had been to the Colburn's home to speak with Lily and met with Violet instead. He had been turned away by the deceased with a threat of the police should he return.

And he had killed her over it.

"I know I am not supposed to be here," I said, trying

to hide the panicked pitch of my voice. I stood up and wiped my fingers over my suddenly clammy forehead. "I just wanted to come and remember Violet. The back door was propped open."

"Yes, I noticed that," he said, moving towards me slowly. An entire room separated us, but I felt crowded already. I didn't want him moving any closer to me. "I saw the door open from the alley and came to investigate who might be inside."

"Just me," I said as calmly as I could.

How did I not notice the predatory look in the waiter's eyes that night? The careful way he moved as though every expression and step was choreographed?

I'd considered every possibility except the most obvious. Because our waiter had been friendly. He'd rushed over to help when Violet collapsed. He'd stayed later than all of the other staff to bring me, Dorothy, and Virginia drinks, to comfort us while we dealt with the tragedy.

It had all been a ruse. A way for the waiter to divert suspicion.

And I had fallen for it.

"Would you like me to escort you out?" he asked, sliding his hands into the pockets of his coat. A chill ran down my spine as he continued, "I'm sure the police would not appreciate either of us being here. It is an active investigation, after all."

I could not tell him no because I was not supposed to be in the restaurant at all. He would not simply turn around and leave. And even if he did, I would be too afraid to follow after him, worried he'd be waiting to attack me in the alley.

I also could not accept his offer for the same reason.

So, I stood there, frozen and terrified.

"Miss?" he asked, face creased in false concern. "Are you all right? Should I send for someone?"

"Yes," I said quickly. "A doctor. I feel ill."

I needed another person here. Someone to ensure the waiter would not attack me. Someone who could ensure I would get out of the restaurant alive and able to get to the police.

"There is a doctor just down the street," he said, extending an arm, beckoning me towards him. "I will walk you."

There was no way out. Not through the front door or the back.

There was no one to hear me scream.

Panic gripped my chest, making it hard to breathe.

"You can trust me," he said, moving closer without ever giving me a clear shot at the kitchen door—at escape.

"I don't even know your name." That was true. If I'd bothered to look into the staff at the restaurant and paid closer attention to Lily's story of love unrequited, I might have connected the dots. But I hadn't, and now I was paying the price for my oversight.

The waiter bowed playfully at the waist. "Samuel Fisher at your service, Miss."

Samuel Fisher. If I ever made it out of the restaurant, that would be the name I would give to the police. If I didn't make it out, that would also be the name of the man who killed me.

Hopefully someone else would uncover what I had failed to discover until it was too late.

"I would rather wait here, Samuel," I said, laying a hand to my forehead. "I feel faint. I don't think I can walk."

"I will help you," he said, one hand still extended towards me, the other hidden in his coat pocket. "I will not let you fall."

I looked at his hand as though it were a snake slithering towards me on the ground. I was out of excuses. I had to either take his hand and my chances or run.

Samuel moved closer to me. A dark hat was pulled low over his eyes, but I could see them watching me, narrowed, confused. He flexed his fingers, taking another step until we were only an arm's length apart.

When he picked up his foot to move again, I ran.

I darted to the left around the near table and sprinted for the kitchen door.

If I could get through the door and to the alley, maybe I could scream for help. Maybe I could get someone's attention.

Maybe Samuel would be too afraid to attack me in public, and he would let me go.

I was running full tilt towards the door when, suddenly, Samuel was standing between me and escape.

He had come around from the other direction, and he was much faster than me.

I slammed to a stop against the edge of a table, knocking a few of the chairs onto the floor, and then scrambled back to put more distance between us again.

My heart jostled around in my chest, and I tried to take deep breaths to keep myself from fainting.

Samuel fisted his hands at his side and pressed his lips together, shaking his head. "I hoped you wouldn't make this more difficult than necessary. I hoped you would come with me and allow me to make this easy for you."

"Make what easy?" I asked, the words breathless.

He tilted his head to the side. "Your death."

I gasped, and Samuel frowned. Though, there was also amusement sparking in his eyes. A kind of pleasure at my fear.

"I saw you at Lily's house," he said. "Twice. Once you even bumped into me, and I thought that would be it. You'd know it was me. But you didn't notice me. None of you wealthy women notice anyone but yourselves."

"I did notice you," I argued. "I noticed your jacket, but I did not see your face. Your jacket is the reason I knew it was you when you walked through the door."

"You may be slightly more observant than your peers," he allowed with a shrug. "But it will not save your life now."

"Why did you come here? Did you follow me?" I asked.

He snorted. "No, I did not follow you. I have better things to do with my time, though I'm sure you wouldn't believe that. I came here because—"

He stopped, and for the first time since he'd walked through the kitchen door, I sensed hesitation. Samuel tucked his hand back in his pocket. "It does not matter."

"You are going to kill me, aren't you?" I asked.

He nodded slowly.

"Then tell me," I said with a shrug. "There is no sense in keeping your secrets now. I'll be dead soon."

Samuel chewed on the inside of his cheek, mulling

over my suggestion. Then, suddenly, a grin split his face wide. "I had to come back for the poison."

He dug in his pocket and pulled out a small glass vial filled with a white powder.

"The police never found it in all of their searching. I tried to take it with me the night of Violet Colburn's death, but it had been moved from the hiding place where I'd left it. At first, I thought someone had figured out what it was and turned it over to the police, but then I saw an officer pull open the spice cabinet, and there it was. My small vial mixed in amongst the other glass jars."

"Someone moved it to the spice rack?" I asked.

He nodded, laughing softly to himself. "An oblivious fellow worker, I assume. Even though I knew where it was, I did not have an opportunity to retrieve it before the restaurant was closed. Then, the police were guarding the place day and night. I was sure they'd find it, but they didn't. I received the notice this morning that the restaurant would reopen in two days because the police finished their search last night. They found nothing."

My heart sank.

Nothing. Days of searching did not return any information. If Samuel killed me, it was likely no one would ever know.

"How?" I said, my voice almost a whisper. "Didn't they interview Violet's family?"

"Family? Yes," he said. "Staff? No."

No one had spoken to Lily, and Lily would not seek them out. She had not made the connection between Samuel and Violet. How, I would never understand. I'd imagined her to be a bright, if naïve, young woman. Now,

I knew she was simple. A silly girl who worshipped Violet and didn't have a serious thought in her head.

And she was the person who would hold the key to my murder.

"Lily is a beautiful girl," Samuel said. "Young and lovely and sweet. She never would have refused me if it had not been for Violet. She poisoned Lily against me. She whispered lies in her ear and told her I was not serious about her."

"You loved her?" I asked.

Samuel's mouth opened and closed. "Well, I'm not sure I would say that yet, but I cared for her deeply. I wanted to take care of her."

"You killed a woman over another woman you did not even love?" I asked in disbelief.

"No," Samuel shouted. "I killed her for besmirching my good name. For spreading lies about me."

I recalled what Lily had told me. "Violet told her you flirted with other women. She said she saw you talking with different women often."

"Is that a crime?" he asked. "Lily and I were not together yet. There was no reason for me to stop talking to other women altogether. I would have, though. If she had chosen me, I would have devoted myself to her."

"Violet did not besmirch your name, then. She told the truth, and you killed her."

Samuel growled. "You've already made up your mind about me, it seems. So, there is no sense in arguing."

"I've made up my mind about you because you killed my friend," I said.

"She kept Lily away from me, and for that, she deserved to pay."

"Death is a steep price," I said.

Samuel shrugged. "It seemed fair to me."

He reached into his other pocket and pulled out a knife. I gasped, and he smiled at my surprise. "I left threats at her home. In her car. On her bedroom window. Small slips of paper with ominous messages written on them. *I see you. I know what you've done. You can't hide.*"

I shivered. Violet must have been terrified. It was no wonder she was on edge. Those notes had been appearing in her life, and she had no idea who was sending them.

"Then, I simply waited until I saw Philip Carlisle's name on the reservation list. I'd seen how she followed that man everywhere, appearing here at the restaurant whenever he did. When his name appeared on the list, I knew Violet would come in that day, as well. So, the only thing left was to decide how I wanted to do it."

He ran the blade of the knife across his thumb nail, eyes tracing the path of the knife over his skin. "I could not attack her in a restaurant full of people. I could not set a fire or have her be hit by a car. It had to be something subtle, something that would not happen right away. Something that would take time. Naturally, I settled on poison."

Naturally. As though any normal human would have settled on the same idea. As though it was not entirely beyond belief that he had resorted to murder to deal with his problems.

Samuel Fisher was dangerously delusional.

"Violet was seated in my section, I slipped the poison into her drink, and then I waited."

"What if she had shared her drink with someone at

the table?" I asked. "Or if it had been delivered to the wrong person? What if you mixed up the drink orders?"

Samuel shrugged. "I hoped that wouldn't happen."

Dangerous. Dangerous. Dangerous.

The word radiated through me like a heartbeat. This man had no conscience, no soul. He would have killed anyone with no remorse at all, seeing no error in his ways.

"And it didn't," he continued. "My poison found its intended target, I am going to get rid of the only person who knows I am guilty, and there will be nothing standing between myself and Lily."

"I'm not the only person who knows," I said quickly. "I have a partner. Someone who helped me investigate Violet's death. He knows your name and—"

Samuel shook his head. "Valiant effort, Miss, but you already admitted you only recognized me by my coat."

I tried a different tactic.

"Do you really think Lily will want to be with the man who murdered her friend?" I asked. "She loved Violet like a sister, and you killed her."

"Who is going to tell her?" he asked. "You certainly won't, as I plan for you to be dead within the next few minutes."

There was only one table separating us. Ten steps between me and death.

I could run for the front of the restaurant, but I would have to hurl myself through the front window to escape, and even if I did, I was not entirely confident it would break on the first attempt. The glass was thick, and I did not have time for a failed escape.

No, it had to be the back door. I had to get past him and run into the alley.

Or fight.

Samuel had a knife, and I had nothing.

There wasn't even a butter knife on the tables. Nothing I could use to defend myself except for the furniture. So, before Samuel could take another step, I grabbed one of the chairs from the table and held it out in front of me.

After only a few seconds, my arms began to shake from the weight. I could barely hold it up, so how was I going to swing it and do any kind of damage? Still, I couldn't show him my weakness. Couldn't give up yet.

Samuel smiled. "Are you going to fight me? I wish you wouldn't. It will be better for you if you turn yourself over. Better even than Violet's death. She had to collapse and seize. It really was a gruesome death, wasn't it?"

He would know. I could see Samuel rushing over, a perfect mask of concern and horror on his face. He had pressed his fingers to where Violet's pulse had stopped beating. Now, I realized he had only done this to be certain she was dead. Because he wanted to get confirmation.

Samuel took a step to his left, and I mirrored his movement to my right. As soon as he realized the move put me closer to the kitchen door, however, he backtracked, reclaiming his previous position. I did the same.

He sighed. "This dance is unnecessary. We both know I will outrun you."

"Would you like to wager?" I asked. "I will wager my life you can't outrun me. Give me a two second head start."

Samuel surprised me by laughing. "You are funny. I don't understand at all why you were friends with Violet Carlisle. An awful girl."

Before the words were even out of his mouth, Samuel jumped onto the table in one fluid motion and sprinted towards me.

I screamed, threw the chair away, and dove to the side.

I heard and felt his feet slam into the floor as I scrambled to mine. Just as I'd found the ground beneath me again and was moving to run, Samuel reached out and grabbed my ankle.

His fingers were icy cold, and he yanked hard, tearing my leg out from underneath me.

I reached for the table leg closest, trying to find anything to resist, but the table simply moved with me. So, I began to kick.

On the second swing of my leg, the heel of my shoe connected with Samuel's nose.

He shouted and lost his grip, allowing me to crawl out of his arm's reach.

I looked down and saw blood on my shoe and then saw Samuel clutching his face, blood oozing between his fingers.

"You'll pay for that," he growled.

He lifted the knife and lunged towards me, but I rolled out of the way. He lunged again, and I lifted my leg and kicked him in the chest.

Though, not before his blade caught me.

There was too much happening to be aware of anything aside from the pain and the warm ooze of blood.

I screamed and kicked again, but this time, Samuel caught my foot in his hands.

He stood up, still holding onto my ankle, and reached out for my other leg. I swung my leg in wide, circling arcs, trying to keep it out of his reach. Samuel gritted his teeth and on the third attempt, as my leg was growing tired, he grabbed my ankle.

He locked my legs together with both of his hands and began dragging me across the floor to where, I realized, he'd dropped his knife.

When he'd stabbed me, I must have knocked it from his hands.

"No, no," I screamed, thrashing my body as hard as I could, but it didn't seem to matter. Samuel was stronger than I was and my fighting barely made a difference at all.

"Don't fight," he grunted, trying to keep control of me. He loosened his grip on my legs slightly as he reached over for the knife on the floor, but he grabbed me quickly when I tried to slip out of his hold. "You are making it worse for yourself."

If Samuel managed to get to his knife, that would be the end for me. I wouldn't survive. He would kill me and drag my body somewhere, and no one would ever hear from me again.

I couldn't stop fighting.

I sat up and swung my arm, trying to hit him with my fist. My knuckled grazed the end of his nose but it wasn't enough to knock him back or make him loosen his grip.

Then, all at once, Samuel dropped my legs and lunged away from me. I scooted backwards a tiny bit before he was on top of me again, his knees on either side of my waist, pinning me to the floor.

I saw the knife in his hand.

This was it.

He had the knife, and I couldn't defend myself. Couldn't stop him.

I was going to die.

Samuel lifted the knife over his shoulder, eyes wild and determined. I squeezed my eyes shut, and there was a loud crunching sound.

I imagined it was the sound of the knife cutting through me, tearing through my bones and muscles, and I hoped it would be over quickly.

Then, Samuel fell on top of me.

I screamed, but the sound was cut off when Samuel's weight landed on me, pressing the air from my lungs.

I gasped for air, but couldn't find any. And Samuel wasn't moving.

His body was limp and lifeless on top of mine.

I tried to run my hand across my body to feel if he'd stabbed me, but I didn't think he had.

So, what had happened?

"Alice?"

The voice startled me, and I screamed again before a figure popped up over Samuel's shoulder.

Sherborne Sharp.

He dropped down to his knees and rolled Samuel over onto his back. Then, he grabbed my hand and yanked me to my feet. Sherborne ran his hands across my face and shoulders, assessing me.

"Are you hurt, Alice? Are you all right?"

I looked down to see blood dripping down my leg, but I could stand on it. No serious damage had been done.

I nodded, my heart still leaping in my chest. "Yes. I'm all right."

All at once, I realized how strange it was that Sherborne Sharp was standing in front of me.

"What are you doing here?" I asked, looking around.

Then, I saw it.

A frying pan on the floor next to Samuel Fisher's unconscious body.

"You hit him." It was a statement, not a question. "How?"

"Really hard," Sherborne said drily. Then, he sighed and shook his head. "I was heading back to your house to speak with you, and I saw you walking away. So, I followed. I lost you a couple blocks away, but I guessed where you were going. When I got to the alley and saw the spoon in the door, I guessed you were inside, so I waited outside to keep watch. Then, I heard you scream."

"You were keeping watch for me?" I asked.

He twisted his lips to the side and nodded. "I should have come in sooner. That was too close. He almost—"

"He didn't," I said, laying a hand on Sherborne's arm.

He looked down where my hand landed, and after a few seconds, I pulled it away and turned back towards Samuel.

"We have to call for the police before he wakes up," I said. "He killed Violet. He poisoned her. Lily as good as told me who the killer was, but I didn't listen. I got fixated on my theories and didn't look at the person right in front of me. I can't believe I was so stupid and—"

"Breathe, Alice," Sherborne said, putting a hand on

my lower back and pushing me towards the kitchen. "This isn't your fault."

He led me outside, reminding me to inhale every time my emotions threatened to overwhelm me, and then before I knew it, the police had arrived.

They dragged Samuel Fisher still unconscious from the restaurant and put him in the back of a police car.

I was so busy being interviewed and examined by a doctor that I didn't keep track of where Sherborne was. Later, when I finished and went to look for him, to apologize and thank him, he had already left.

17

The wound to my leg ended up being a shallow gash that simply needed to be bandaged and kept clean. Still, shallow or not, it hurt with every step and my mother insisted I be housebound for several days.

"Do you need anything?" my mother asked for the third time in an hour. "I can send for some more tea."

"I couldn't drink another drop. Really, I'm fine," I insisted.

The stairs were manageable, but I winced the first time I tried to mount them, and blankets, pillows, and books were immediately carried down from my room to the sitting room. I was certainly well enough to be back in my room, but I'd kind of taken to the attention being stationed in the sitting room gave me. Plus, if I had to be partially bedridden, I didn't want to be shut away alone in my room. It would have been boring.

My mother leaned against the door and smiled at me,

though I could see a tinge of sadness in it. "I am so glad you are all right, Alice."

"Me too."

"I mean it," she scolded. "You frightened the life out of me, showing up here with a police escort and a physician. I had no idea what was going on."

"I'm fine," I repeated. "Really. I'm sorry I frightened you, but everything is all right now."

She sighed. "I hope so. I just hate to leave you like this."

"No," I said a bit too loudly. "Please don't cancel on my account. The maids will take excellent care of me."

For the first time in weeks, my mother was planning to attend a social engagement with my father. Some birthday party for an acquaintance of his. I wasn't certain, I only knew my parents were going to leave the house together, which had not happened in a very long time. I would never have forgiven myself if I'd been the reason my mother stayed in.

"I know," she said. "But I'm your mother. I should be here."

"And you will be. *After* your party."

My mother rushed forward and planted a kiss on my forehead, wiping away residual lipstick from my forehead, and then hurried upstairs to finish getting ready. Twenty minutes later, my parents left together, arm in arm, and I waved to them from the couch.

As soon as they were gone, I tried to open my book and occupy myself that way, but just as they had been for days, my thoughts kept going back to Sherborne Sharp.

I had not seen him since the heroic rescue. No visit or letter to check on my recovery.

I just wanted to see him. To thank him and apologize for blackmailing him. No other reason came to mind.

So, when a knock sounded at the door shortly after my parents left, I jumped up, wincing at the pain in my thigh, and moved towards the door. I waved away a maid, insisting I'd answer it myself, and flattened down my pale cotton dress before answering the door.

"Alice!" Virginia and Dorothy rushed forward in unison, pulling me into a hug.

I stumbled back in surprise and then patted their backs. "Hello, girls. I wasn't expecting a visit."

"We've been terrible friends," Dorothy said, straightening her hat over her red curls.

"Dreadful," Virginia agreed, twisting her thin lips to one side of her mouth.

"It's fine," I said, not entirely certain what I was forgiving them for. "I haven't been up for visitors before today anyway."

"Not that," Dorothy said, waving a hand as though dismissing what I'd just said. "We should have been here before the attack. After Violet's murder. We should have spoken to you."

I frowned. "I didn't reach out to you, either. Why does that make you a horrible friend?"

Virginia pushed Dorothy into the entryway, closed the door, and then led us all towards the sitting room. The two women took up chairs across from my sofa and Dorothy continued her explanation.

"We did not reach out to you because we thought you may have killed Violet," Dorothy admitted, her cheeks flaming the same color red as her hair.

Her admission surprised me so much that I actually

smiled. "Did you really?"

Virginia nodded in solemn agreement. "We thought you had killed Violet because...well, because—"

"Because Violet told us not to speak with you anymore," Dorothy blurted out. She sighed with apparent relief once the words were out and then took a deep breath to continue. "When your brother went to prison for murder, Violet said we would damage our social standing by being seen with you. She suggested we all keep our distance, and we listened."

"Oh." As the shock wore off, I began to think back over that time. When the news first broke, Dorothy came to see me. She hugged me and let me talk to her when I didn't feel like I could talk to anyone else.

Virginia offered me solace in the form of distraction. She complained about her parents and school and helped me forget my life had turned upside down for an hour or so at a time.

And then, they stopped.

There were excuses at first and then no contact at all. I'd written it off as growing older and growing apart, but to hear that Violet had been behind it all from the start hurt in a way I didn't expect.

"You can be angry with us," Virginia said. "If things were reversed, I would be livid."

I thought about it for a moment and then shook my head. "I'm not angry."

"You should be," Dorothy said, near tears. "We were terrible friends."

"So was I," I said with a shrug. "Once you stopped talking to me, I didn't even try. I let our friendship fade away without even a fight. So, I can't blame you for everything."

They both nodded, looking solemn.

"And I can't be angry with Violet," I said. "She's dead."

There was a brief moment of silence, and then Virginia let out a small chuckle. "I'm sorry. It's not funny, but I mean...it is a little funny. Isn't that just like something Violet would do? Die rather than face the consequences of her actions."

We all nodded in agreement, stifling our inappropriate laughter. Quickly the conversation turned serious again.

"Reginald saw you at the restaurant several days after," Dorothy said. "When he told me, I was certain you'd done it. I feel so foolish now, but at the time, grief and confusion and fear—I allowed my imagination to run away with me."

"I never even considered the two of you as possibilities," I said. "Though, I also never considered the waiter. Perhaps, that is why Violet wanted me to connect her with my cousin Rose."

"Rose Prideaux?" Virginia asked. "Why?"

I explained what I'd learned from Samuel Fisher. I told them about Violet interfering with Samuel and Lily and about the threatening notes he had been leaving her.

"After her death, I found a note in my purse. Violet wanted me to put her in contact with my cousin and her detective husband. She wanted someone to help her solve this case, but did not want to take it to the police."

"Maybe if she had, she'd still be alive," Dorothy said.

Virginia shook her head. "I can't believe she called us all together again just to use you to get to your cousin."

I hadn't really thought about it before, but it was rather self-serving. She wouldn't speak to me because my brother was a murderer, but when she was the one in trouble, she ran back to me.

I took a deep breath and let it go. She was gone, murdered for no good reason, and I was alive. Holding a grudge or anger towards her for any reason was pointless.

"It is all in the past," I said, smiling at them both. "I hope we can all move into the future together."

"Absolutely," Dorothy agreed. Virginia nodded in agreement.

Although I had not been seriously injured in the fight with Samuel Fisher, the altercation had left me feeling worn, so it was not long before I politely urged my friends towards the door.

"I will come at the end of the week," Dorothy said, touching her stomach. "Assuming my little one doesn't decide to join us early."

"I'll come next," Virginia said.

I assured them they would both be welcomed to my home any time they wished. When they were on the porch, I had nearly closed the door when Virginia spun around, one finger held up to stop me.

"I nearly forgot," she said. "Reginald told Dorothy you were seen at the restaurant with Sherborne Sharp."

Over Virginia's shoulder, Dorothy drew her brows together in concern. I stared at both women. "Yes, I was."

Virginia nodded, biting her lower lip between her teeth. "I didn't want to leave today without warning you to be careful of the company you keep. At the risk of sounding like Violet, I've heard Mr. Sharp is a less than suitable companion. Especially for a woman of your breeding."

Breeding. As though I were a horse.

I smiled. "I appreciate your concern."

When I tried again to shut the door, Virginia stopped me. "We are only saying this because we care."

"I appreciate that," I said. "I genuinely do. However, he has proven himself a loyal friend to me, and as my friends, I expect you both to respect my decision and my privacy."

Virginia seemed surprised to have been dismissed, but she and Dorothy both nodded in understanding and left.

I stood in the doorway, watching them go, and was about to shut the door for the third time when a shadow in the far right of my vision caught my attention. I turned just as a man moved out of the shade of the house and onto the front steps.

It was Sherborne Sharp.

I laid a hand over my heart and gasped. "You frightened me."

"It was not my intention," he said, though his smile showed he'd found amusement in it. "I was walking up to knock on the door when I saw it open. I thought it might be your parents, so I hid."

I frowned. "If you were going to knock on the door, wouldn't you have seen them anyway?"

"Yes," he admitted, running a hand through his dark hair before putting his hat back on. "I admit there was a flaw in my thinking, but I panicked."

"Well, there is no need. They are both out for the evening. Besides, I told my parents everything. I explained precisely what we've been up to this last week and what happened at the restaurant, and you are now tied for their favorite person in all of London next to King George V."

"Good company to be included with," he said. Then, he tilted his head to the side, one eyebrow raised. "You told them everything?"

I shook my head back and forth playfully. "I may have kept a few details to myself. There are things no one needs to know about. We've both made our fair share of mistakes."

At that, he looked at me, lids heavy.

"I am sorry," I said plainly. "I should not have accused you of having any ill will towards me. You have been honest with me from the start, and I should have trusted you."

Sherborne looked down at the ground, and when he looked up, his mouth was pinched as though he was holding back a smile. In a flash, however, it was gone. "Well, I hope this means I have lived up to my end of the agreement and you won't be manipulating me into any more dangerous situations."

"You are free of our agreement," I said, waving my arm like a queen knighting someone.

"Good," he said. "I don't think I can take any more life and death situations. Saving you this last time was hard enough."

"I'm sorry it was such a burden for you."

His eyes sparked with amusement. "That is quite all right. I suppose the risk was worth the reward in the end."

"You suppose?" I shook my head, biting back a smile.

"Remind me not to count on you the next time I'm being attacked. I want someone who is certain."

"If not me, then who will you count on?" he asked. "Do you have many similar secrets stowed away to be used as blackmail when the need arises?"

"Unfortunately, no. You were the only one."

He nodded and backed down the steps. "Well, in that case, if you do ever find yourself in dire circumstances, feel free to call me. Though, only as a last resort."

"What a generous offer."

Sherborne bowed at the waist. "I am nothing if not generous, Miss Beckingham."

He spun around and walked to the gate, looking back one more time to lift his hand in a wave.

I'd noticed before, but in that moment especially, I couldn't help but see the fine figure Mr. Sharp cut in his suit. Before I could dwell on it too long, he turned and walked down the street. I watched him until he disappeared around the corner, wondering how long it would be until I required his services again.

18

After Virginia, Dorothy, and Sherborne were long gone, the book on my lap remained opened yet unread.

I could not focus my attention on it. Instead, my mind wandered to Edward.

In many ways, he was the cause of all of this.

His crime was my first experience with death up close. Before that, I had been shielded from the darker elements of the world. Even when Rose first came to live with our family, no one told me her parents had been killed until the day she arrived. Before that, I'd been under the impression she was coming for a simple visit rather than to live.

But Edward committed murder while we were on a family holiday. While I slept, innocent and oblivious, several rooms away.

Then, he was sent to prison and murdered there himself, and our family fractured in ways I didn't think we'd ever survive.

Except, we did.

Catherine and I were closer than we ever were before, and I felt as though I knew my parents better. Seeing them experience that kind of grief and loss helped me realize they were people, too.

The only person I was no closer to than before was Edward. If anything, he seemed more mysterious to me.

What had led him to the thought of murder?

Hearing Samuel Fisher explain the motive behind his crimes made me realize what kind of crazed person it would take to kill someone. No rational person would be angry enough to resort to taking a life.

Yet, Edward had always been rational.

He had always been level-headed and reasonable and logical. He was like our father in that way.

So, what happened?

And why was he killed?

I wanted to believe the police had told us the truth, and Edward was killed in a prison fight, but more and more, that story didn't make any sense.

Why had Edward been the only one to die? Why were more injuries not reported?

Catherine's theory that a villain called the Chess Master had something to do with Edward's descent into the criminal realm and, ultimately, his death, seemed more and more likely. Though, I had no idea where to start looking for confirmation.

Then, I realized what I needed to do.

I pushed myself up from the couch and, for the first time in days, climbed the stairs to my room. The cut in my thigh pulled uncomfortably, but I made it without incident and moved quickly down the hallway and straight to the desk in my room. I pulled out my paper and a pen.

Violet had left a note asking me to reach out to Rose and Achilles for help, but I had ignored her request under the belief that I could handle the investigation on my own.

I did not think the same would be true of my brother's death.

Dear Rose,

I have much to tell you, most of which I will have to save for another letter. If Mama writes to you with the news before I can, please do not be upset with me. I am of a single mind right now, only able to focus on one thing:

Who is The Chess Master?

When Edward died, I was a young girl. You spared me details because I was a child, but I am no longer a child. I am a woman, and I want to know what happened to my brother. Catherine told me you may know more than you've said, so I'm reaching out to implore you to tell me what you know. The more I sit with my thoughts and feelings on Edward's crime and his death, things do not add up. There are unanswered questions that, if you do not answer, I will seek out elsewhere.

Again, forgive me for being short, but this letter is urgent. I hope you will respond to it promptly and honestly.

All my love dear cousin,

Alice

I folded the letter and then leaned back in my chair, staring out of the dark window ahead.

Night had fallen in full force, blanketing the city in swarthy shadows.

As a girl, the dark had never frightened me as it did other children. I had been young and naïve, under the impression that regardless of what lurked outside, I was safe in my room.

In the years since, however, I had learned the truth.

Danger lived everywhere.

In your city and your home. Even in the darkness just beyond your window.

There were no walls too high for it to climb or windows too strong for it to break.

The only thing that could be done was to be prepared for it to come. With this letter to Rose, I hoped that was what I was doing: preparing myself.

Did the Chess Master truly exist? Was he still lurking in the darkness of London, waiting for another opportunity to prey on an ordinary man?

That was what Edward had been, wasn't it? An ordinary man?

He always seemed like one to me. Now, I couldn't be certain. Hopefully, I would find out.

I stood up, and as I did, a shadow appeared to shift at the base of the house. I leaned forward at once to look again, but there was no movement. As I studied the dark grass, a shiver worked its way down my back and raised the hairs on my neck.

It felt as though I was being watched, and I quickly

pulled the curtains closed, double-checking the latch on the window was locked.

The question of who had murdered Violet Colburn had been answered, but my days of investigating were far from over. My quest for answers about Edward's involvement with the Chess Master could lead me into danger and force me to face truths about my family I did not want to face. Yet, I would not stop searching. Not until the case had been solved.

Tired from the day, I turned out the light next to my bed and crawled beneath the covers. As I lay there, staring up at the ceiling, the blankets pulled to my chin, I listened to the house creak around me. I listened to cars rumble down the street. And the sound of my own heart thudding with life in my chest.

As I drifted into sleep, in the place between wakefulness and dreaming, I felt a breeze move through my room, chilling me to the bone. I cuddled the blankets closer and did not open my eyes, afraid of what I might see if I did.

~

Continue following the mysterious adventures of Alice Beckingham in
"Murder by Candlelight."

ABOUT THE AUTHOR

Blythe Baker is the lead writer behind several popular historical and paranormal mystery series. When Blythe isn't buried under clues, suspects, and motives, she's acting as chauffeur to her children and head groomer to her household of beloved pets. She enjoys walking her dog, lounging in her backyard hammock, and fiddling with graphic design. She also likes binge-watching mystery shows on TV.

To learn more about Blythe, visit her website and sign up for her newsletter at www.blythebaker.com

Made in United States
North Haven, CT
13 February 2024

48703857R00125